"You Have A Very Suspicious Nature," Duke Drawled Lazily.

"You bet I do," Lola snapped.

"My feelings for you are going deeper by the minute," he said, flashing her a smile that she saw as smug.

Lola's anger increased tenfold. "Your only feelings for me are below your belt, so don't try to con me, Duke."

"You're angry."

"I'm not only angry, I don't like you. There's the answer to your question. Are you happy now?"

He chuckled. "I don't think you're a liar, Lola Fanon, so what you're trying to do is con both of us. When a woman kisses back the way you did, she doesn't dislike the man who's holding her."

Damn his sorry soul, he was right.

*Made in Montana: The Fanons—
born and raised in Big Sky country...
and heading for a Montana Wedding!*

Dear Reader,

Cowboys and cops...sexy men with a swagger...just the kind of guys to make your head turn. *That's* what we've got for you this month in Silhouette Desire.

The romance begins when Taggart Jones meets his match in Anne McAllister's wonderful MAN OF THE MONTH, *The Cowboy and the Kid*. This is the latest in her captivating CODE OF THE WEST miniseries. And the fun continues with Mitch Harper in *A Gift for Baby*, the next book in Raye Morgan's THE BABY SHOWER series.

Cindy Gerard has created a dynamic hero in the *very* masculine form of J. D. Hazzard in *The Bride Wore Blue*, book #1 in the NORTHERN LIGHTS BRIDES series. And if rugged rascals are your favorite, don't miss Jake Spencer in Dixie Browning's *The Baby Notion*, which is book #1 of DADDY KNOWS LAST, Silhouette's new cross-line continuity. (Next month, look for Helen R. Myers's *Baby in a Basket* as DADDY KNOWS LAST continues in Silhouette Romance!)

Gavin Cantrell is sure to weaken your knees in *Gavin's Child* by Caroline Cross, part of the delightful BACHELORS AND BABIES promotion. And Jackie Merritt—along with hero Duke Sheridan—kicks off her MADE IN MONTANA series with *Montana Fever*.

Heroes to fall in love with—and love scenes that will make your toes curl. That's what Silhouette Desire is all about. Until next month—enjoy!

All the best,

Lucia Macro

Senior Editor

Please address questions and book requests to:
Silhouette Reader Service
U.S.: 3010 Walden Ave., P.O. Box 1325, Buffalo, NY 14269
Canadian: P.O. Box 609, Fort Erie, Ont. L2A 5X3

JACKIE MERRITT
MONTANA FEVER

SILHOUETTE Desire®
Published by Silhouette Books
America's Publisher of Contemporary Romance

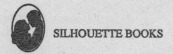 SILHOUETTE BOOKS

ISBN 0-373-76014-0

MONTANA FEVER

Printed in U.S.A.

Books by Jackie Merritt

Silhouette Desire

Big Sky Country #466
Heartbreak Hotel #551
Babe in the Woods #566
Maggie's Man #587
Ramblin' Man #605
Maverick Heart #622
Sweet on Jessie #642
Mustang Valley #664
The Lady and the Lumberjack #683
Boss Lady #705
Shipwrecked! #721
Black Creek Ranch #740
A Man Like Michael #757
Tennessee Waltz #774
Montana Sky #790
Imitation Love #813
Wrangler's Lady #841
Mystery Lady #849
Persistent Lady #854
Nevada Drifter #866
Accidental Bride #914
Hesitant Husband #935
Rebel Love #965
Assignment: Marriage #980
+*Montana Fever* #1014

*The Saxon Brothers
+Made in Montana

Silhouette Special Edition

A Man and a Million #988

Silhouette Books

Summer Sizzlers 1994
"Stranded"

Montana Mavericks

*The Widow and the
  Rodeo Man* #2
The Rancher Takes a Wife #5

JACKIE MERRITT

and her husband live just outside of Las Vegas, Nevada. An accountant for many years, Jackie has happily traded numbers for words. Next to family, books are her greatest joy. She started writing in 1987 and her efforts paid off in 1988 with the publication of her first novel. When she's not writing or enjoying a good book, Jackie dabbles in watercolor painting and likes playing the piano in her spare time.

Prologue

A modest blue sedan drove slowly into the town of Rocky Ford, Montana. Though it was twilight, the woman behind the wheel tried to see everything she passed. Her heart was pounding and had seemingly changed positions in her chest, feeling as though it had risen to the base of her throat.

Her mind and body seemed heavy with unnerving questions. Had she done the right thing by coming here? Maybe she should have written first. Or called.

But no, she thought then. Her goal could not have been accomplished through the mail or by telephone. She had been compelled to come to this place since the moment she had learned the truth, and she must see it through.

Turning her thoughts, she began looking for a motel, something quiet yet busy enough that her presence would pass unnoticed. How long she would be renting a room was an unknown at this point. She might have to change addresses several times to remain anonymous in a town of less than eight thousand residents if things didn't happen fast.

Fortunately, she noted with some relief while traversing the main street, Rocky Ford was not lacking in motels.

Spotting a pleasant-looking redbrick establishment with exceptionally clean grounds and a sign advertising a connecting café, she turned into the parking area and stopped near the office.

Drawing a deep breath to calm her speeding pulse, she got out of her car and walked into the office.

One

Giving her hair a pat, Lola Fanon smiled at herself in the mirror over the sink in the small bathroom of her store. She really liked her new style. Her almost black hair had always been long, at least shoulder-length, and this short but sophisticated cut was a major change.

But she relished change, she thought with another smile. Her reflection seemed to agree. Her green eyes shone with a dancing excitement, precisely the way she felt inside. The store had been open for only three months and was already proving to be a smart decision. And the Lord knew that Lola Fanon, world traveler, settling down—back in her hometown yet—*and* opening a men's clothing store, was definitely a change.

In her mind this innovation was permanent, though. She had finally seen enough of the world and had gotten very lonesome for home. Lonesome for Rocky Ford, Montana, and for her family. It was great to be back, great to be living under her Uncle Charlie's roof again, and it was especially gratifying to be the owner of a business.

Humming under her breath, Lola took her purse and left the little bathroom. Betty Drake, one of her part-time employees, was at the counter ringing up a sale. Lola darted into her office at the back of the store, deposited her purse in a desk drawer, then returned to the main part of the store to walk among the merchandise, her eye attuned to anything out of order. Betty was chatting with her customer—she knew almost everyone who came in—and Lola began straightening the stacks of jeans on the twenty-percent markdown table which the customer had obviously gone through quite thoroughly.

The man left with his packages. The two women smiled at each other as Betty came around the counter. "Good sale. He bought three pairs of jeans and two shirts."

"Great," Lola said. Betty was a wife and mother, and her hours were from an eight o'clock opening until 1:30 p.m. Monday through Friday, as she wanted to be free when her three children got home from school. Lola's help in the afternoons and on Saturdays—the store was closed Sundays—consisted of high school kids, who were proving to be very good help. Lola got along with all of her part-time employees, but she especially enjoyed Betty, who was only a few years older than herself and had a wry sense of humor that sometimes had Lola in stitches.

A woman came in and Betty walked off to greet her. Lola was finishing with the jeans just as the bell above the door jangled again, announcing another customer. She turned from the table with a smile and felt the strangest frisson of energy travel her spine. The man walking in was one for the books, tall, lean and startlingly handsome. A shock of sandy hair. Tanned face. She couldn't see his eyes, as they were behind a pair of very dark sunglasses. He was dressed like most of her male customers, in jeans, boots and Western-cut shirt; nothing unusual, but there was something besides his good looks that affected Lola.

She didn't take time to wonder about it; instead, she began moving toward him. "Good morning."

Duke Sheridan turned his head to see who had spoken to him, at the same time removing his dark glasses and tucking them into his shirt pocket. One good look at Lola had him feeling very male and high-spirited. She was slender, in white jeans and a loosely structured, emerald green blouse tucked into the waistband of the pants. Her dark hair was short and perfect for her beautiful face. Yes, he thought, beautiful. Who was she? Before walking in here he had believed that he'd known every attractive woman in the area.

Every attractive *unattached* woman, he quickly amended; she must be taken.

Not that he was a womanizer. But he'd lived in this part of Montana all his life and there were very few unfamiliar faces.

"Morning," he replied with a lopsided grin that arrowed straight to the core of Lola's system. "Been meaning to stop in since this store opened." They had gotten close enough to each other for him to see the name tag on Lola's blouse. He bent his head to read it aloud. "Lola Fanon." His eyes rose to meet hers. "Are you one of Charlie Fanon's kids?" The Fanon on her name tag was encouraging. Most married women took their husband's last name.

"You know Charlie?"

"Everyone knows Charlie. Let's see. He has three kids, if I remember right. Haven't seen any of them for quite a while, now that I think about it."

"He has two children and a niece," Lola said with a small laugh of indulgence. "I'm the niece."

One of Duke's eyebrows went up. "Really? I was always under the impression that...well, you know what I mean."

"A lot of people thought Charlie was my father while I was growing up. Some probably still do."

Duke's gaze kept roaming her features. Her perfect little nose, startling green eyes and sensual mouth seemed to demand a great deal of study. He was thoroughly enjoying this unexpected meeting, and was willing to talk about anything to prolong it.

He folded his arms across his chest, as though settling in for a good long chat. "So, Charlie raised you?"

"Since I was nine."

"But we've never met, have we?"

"Not that I can recall." That wasn't completely true. He seemed vaguely familiar, although she couldn't really place him. There was hordes of information she could pass on to clarify her own past for this man, but it really wasn't any of his business, good-looking or not. "Is there something I can help you find?" she asked, indicating the merchandise in the store with a wave of her hand.

He smiled. "You know, maybe there is. Seems like I lost *something* when I walked in here."

"Pardon?"

"Yeah, there seems to be an empty spot right about here." Unfolding his arms, he tapped the left side of his chest. "I think what's missing is a piece of my heart. Do you have it?"

Lola's face colored. What an outrageous flirt! Well, she'd dealt with his sort before.

"I think if you're suddenly missing a body part, sport, it's from a little higher up than your chest," she said pertly.

Duke laughed with genuine relish. He did like a woman with spirit. "Could you by any chance be referring to my brain, Lola Fanon? Oh, by the way, I'm Duke Sheridan." He held out his right hand.

Lola stared at it. Now she knew who he was, or at least, *what* he was. A rancher. The Sheridan Ranch was one of the largest and most successful in the area. Or it had been before she left Rocky Ford.

But did she want to touch that big masculine hand? Feel its warmth? Physically connect the two of them, if only for a handshake? Although Betty was taking good care of her lady customer, Lola could sense that she was also highly interested in what was happening near the table of jeans.

"Hey," Duke said softly. "Don't be afraid to shake my hand. I guarantee not to bite."

Lola tilted her chin to a defiant angle, and she boldly stared into Duke's golden brown eyes while she laid her hand in his.

He laughed. "I don't scare you at all, do I?"

"Not an iota." But she only allowed the handshake to last a few seconds. "Now, is there anything I can show you, Mr. Sheridan?"

"A whole lot, Miss Fanon, if you're willing."

His bedroom voice sent ripples of heat throughout her body, which she did her best to ignore. "I'm willing and delighted to show you anything in the store that's for sale, Mr. Sheridan. The key phrase is *for sale,* in case you missed it."

"Didn't miss it at all." Grinning to himself, Duke walked over to a display of hats. "You've got some good merchandise in here." He took a hat from the rack and put it on. "What do you think?"

"It's definitely you," she drawled, which was an out-and-out lie. The black hat he'd chosen was huge, with a ten-inch crown and a wide, floppy brim, and it looked ridiculous on him.

He laughed as though she'd said something hilarious. Removing the hat, he replaced it on the rack and picked up another, a cream-colored Stetson. "I think I like this one."

So did she. "The black one suits you much better," she said with a smile of exaggerated sweetness.

"Yeah, right." Leaving the hat on, he moved to a rack of shirts. Flipping through them, he asked, "Who owns the store?"

"I do."

He sent her a glance. "So you're a businesswoman. Or should I say businessperson?"

She shrugged. "Say anything you wish."

He stopped to give her a long look. "That's an opening if I ever heard one. Do you mean it?"

"I'm talking about my title, Mr. Sheridan."

"Duke. I've decided to call you Lola, so you may as well call me Duke."

"Male logic. Now why doesn't that surprise me?"

"Maybe you don't surprise easily." His smile flashed. "Then again, it could be that you're feeling as overwhelmed by me as I am by you."

"Oh, please," she said, attempting a contemptuous intonation. "Men do not overwhelm me, Mr. Sheridan."

"Not even once in a while?" he said teasingly, at the same time pulling three shirts from the circular rack. "I'll take these, along with the hat," he said before she could respond to his silly question.

Lola accepted the shirts, genuinely surprised that he was planning to buy something.

"And these two," he said, adding another two shirts to the three she was holding.

"Would you like to try them on?" she asked.

"Don't need to. They'll fit. Let's see what else you've got in here." He walked over to the jeans section, which was in a different location than the table of jeans at the front of the store. With his hands on his hips, he perused the laden shelves. "Good size selection. Little guys, big guys..." He gave her a grin. "They can all buy here."

"That's the idea." His grins were much too adorable for Lola's comfort. And yet she found herself waiting for the next one. She enjoyed flirting with an outstanding guy as much as any woman, but there was the strangest little voice in the back of her mind issuing warnings. If she remembered anything at all about the Sheridans, father and son, it was the rumors that they always got what they wanted, when they wanted it. It was entirely possible that Duke flirted with every reasonably attractive woman he ran across, just as he was doing with her, so she shouldn't allow herself to get too giddy about it.

"I'll bring these shirts to the counter while you look around," she told him. "Would you like me to take the hat, too?"

"Thanks, but I like it right where it is."

"Fine." Lola walked across the store to the counter and hung the shirts on a rack behind it.

Betty excused herself momentarily from her customer and hurried over. "Do you know who he is?" she asked in an undertone.

"He introduced himself. I remember the name, but not him."

"He's the best catch in the county," Betty whispered. "Be nice." Smiling broadly, she returned to her customer.

Lola could see Duke pulling jeans from a shelf; apparently he had found his size. After a deep breath, she walked back to him. "These jeans are—"

"No salesmanship necessary. I'll take four pair."

"Oh."

"I see you carry boots." Duke started for the boot display.

"Not many, Mr. Sheridan. I plan to expand the shoe and boot department, but at the present my stock is limited."

"These are good." He picked up a gray lizard boot and looked it over. "Got this one in a size twelve?"

"I think... possibly. Let me check." Hurrying to the storage room, she scanned the boot boxes. Elated, she returned with a size twelve. "Sit down. You really must try boots on. They vary a great deal depending on style and brand, and boots should fit perfectly."

"Really?"

She flushed slightly. He'd worn boots all his life, for heaven's sake, and certainly didn't need advice on how they should fit.

"Sorry," he said. "Only teasing. I like it when you blush." Duke sat in one of the three chairs Lola had installed in the boot section of the store. "Are you going to put them on me?"

"No, you are." So, he liked making her blush. For some reason that annoyed her. She opened the box and pulled out the boots, removing the packing from inside them. "Here you are," she said, placing the boots on the floor next to the ones on his feet.

Chuckling quietly, he yanked off his boots and pulled on the new ones. Standing, he checked the result in the mirror. "What do you think?"

"They look great, but how do they feel?"

"Like new boots." He grinned, but only for a moment. With his eyes narrowed on her, he said in a tone too low to reach Betty and the other woman in the store, "You sure are a pretty little thing."

Lola cleared her throat. "Thank you. About the boots..."

"I'd much rather talk about you. How about going next door to the diner with me for a cup of coffee?"

Startled at his unexpected invitation, Lola felt another blush sneaking into her cheeks. "Thanks, but I really can't leave."

"Aw, sure you can. You're the owner, aren't you? You can do anything you want." Duke resumed his seat and pulled off the lizard boots. "I'll take these."

He hadn't asked for the price. "They're $375," Lola said.

He shrugged. "How about that coffee?"

Lola gathered up the boots and fit them back in their box, while Duke pulled on his old boots.

"Sorry," she said. "I really can't leave the store." She heard the phone ringing then, and since the boot department was close to her office, she called to Betty, "I'll get it. Please excuse me, Mr. Sheridan. I won't be long."

"Take your time, sweetheart. I'm in no hurry."

His sassy response caused Lola's pulse to flutter. She had met some intriguing men during college and her years of travel, but none to compare with Duke Sheridan. Leaving the office door ajar, she picked up the phone. "Men's Western Wear, Lola speaking."

"Miss Fanon? This is Naomi Pritchard, the principal of the Lewis and Clark Elementary School. May I speak to Betty, please? I'm afraid we have a bit of an emergency. Her son, Brian, was hurt in a fall. The school nurse thinks he may have broken his arm."

"I'll get her immediately." Dropping the phone, Lola went to the door, then decided against calling clear across the store for Betty. Winding through the merchandise, she approached her instead. "Betty, the school principal is on the phone for you."

Betty's eyes registered alarm, but she spoke calmly to her customer. "Please excuse me, Mrs. Callahan."

"Well, certainly, Betty. I'm through anyway. Lola can ring this up for me."

Mrs. Callahan had picked out a striking silver belt buckle with turquoise insets. As Betty sped away, Lola put the buckle in a little box.

"It's a birthday present for my husband. I'm sure he'll love it," Mrs. Callahan said. "You gift wrap, don't you?"

"Yes, we do," Lola replied. Duke was wandering, she saw with a quick glance in his direction. She rang up the sale on the cash register. Betty came out of the office carrying her purse.

"I have to leave, Lola."

Lola nodded. "I know. Mrs. Pritchard explained. Don't worry about anything here."

Betty was on her way to the door. "See you tomorrow morning."

"Only if everything's all right," Lola called. "And let me know how Brian is."

"Will do." Betty went through the door.

A few minutes later, while wrapping Mrs. Callahan's purchase in pretty green-and-silver paper, Lola heard the bell over the door jangle again. Looking up, she saw Duke leaving. And he was still wearing the Stetson! Frowning, she tried to concentrate on what she was doing. But why would he leave with the hat before paying for it? Had he forgotten he was wearing it?

Lola was still thinking about it, worrying a little, after Mrs. Callahan had gone, when Duke returned with two large disposable cups. He walked up to the counter and handed her one.

"If the mountain won't go to Mohammed, then another plan has to be devised," he said, taking small packets of creamer, sugar and a small stirring stick from his shirt pocket. "I didn't know how you liked it, so I brought a little of everything."

"I like it with cream, thank you." Lola set the cup on the counter, removed the lid and emptied a packet of the creamer into it. Raising the cup to her lips, she looked at Duke, who was looking back with an admiring gleam in his eyes. He would not be easily discouraged, she realized, wondering at the same time if she really wanted to discourage him. Okay, so he came on strong. But wasn't she more flattered than put off by his flagrant interest?

"Betty left in a hurry," he said.

"The school principal called. One of her children took a fall, and the nurse thinks he may have broken his arm."

"It happens with active youngsters. I got a few broken bones growing up." He sipped from his cup. "Did you?"

"No, I never broke anything."

"Except for a few hearts, I'll bet." He grinned.

"Except for a few hearts," she confirmed with a straight face. It wasn't true. She'd never broken any hearts that she knew of, but Duke had apparently placed her in the femme fatale category, and why burst his bubble? Flip that coin, she thought with a sudden wariness. If there was a heart-breaker in this store, it was him. A man with a smile like his and an outrageous flirt, to boot? Oh, yes, definitely a heart breaker.

The "best catch in the county," as Betty had referred to him, was a description usually reserved for a man who had eluding commitment down to a fine art. He would play — oh, yes, he would play — but he would never stay. As attractive as Duke was, as much as she enjoyed his audacity, she must watch her step.

And then, right before her eyes, he became a completely different person. Sipping his coffee, he asked in a voice conveying normal curiosity tinged with concern, "What happened to your parents?"

Lola blinked in surprise. How could he change personalities so quickly?

Though confusion was suddenly rampant in her system, she managed to speak evenly. "They died in a car accident."

"And Charlie brought you home with him?"

"My father was Charlie's only brother. They were very close."

"Tragic. My mother died when I was five, so I barely remember her. Then Dad went about three years ago."

"I'm sorry. After you told me your name, I remembered some vague references to the Sheridan men, father and son."

"Then you know I live on a ranch."

Lola nodded. "Yes, you're a cattle rancher."

His gaze seemed to bore into her. "And you're a store owner. How do you like it?"

"I like it very much."

"But before this, you weren't in Rocky Ford for a long time. Where were you?"

"In college, then too many places to list. I traveled."

"For years?" There was puzzlement in his expression.

"Yes, for years." She had to laugh because he looked so befuddled. "I wasn't on the go every day. I took jobs here and there. I worked in a Paris boutique for eight months, and in a little pastry shop in London for about a year."

"A *world* traveler. I thought you were only talking about the U.S."

"Oh, I saw the U.S., too. Then, about a year ago, I started getting lonesome for home."

"What are you, independently wealthy?" He'd never thought of Charlie Fanon as wealthy, but Lola could have inherited from her parents.

Lola laughed again. "Not anymore. Actually, I was never what you'd call wealthy, but my parents' estate provided enough for my education and some to spare. I grew up dreaming of seeing something of the world, so I did it." She glanced around her store, feeling pride in her decor and good taste. "I had enough money left to open this store."

"But why a men's store? I would think a woman would rather sell pretty clothes to other women." He noticed her amused little half smile. "Wrong assumption, huh?"

"Very wrong." She looked him in the eye. "I like men much better than women, Mr. Sheridan."

He chuckled softly. "I sure do admire your honesty, sweetheart."

"Do you?"

"Absolutely." His outlaw grin returned at full throttle. "Of course, there are a whole passel of other things I admire about you, as well." She felt his gaze linger on her bosom for a few seconds, then slowly travel up to her face. "You are one beautiful lady," he said huskily.

"Flattery will get you nowhere, Mr. Sheridan," she said, an automatic response that denied the truth, noticing that her own voice had gotten a bit husky, too.

"It's not flattery, Miss Fanon. I'm as honest as you are."

"Is that a fact?"

They were staring into each other's eyes. It took Lola a minute to shake the feeling that they were all alone in the world. Even the store had seemed to disappear for a time.

Abruptly, she tore her gaze from his and finished the last of her coffee. "Well, I really must get back to work," she said briskly, dropping her cup into the small trash can next to the counter. "Let's see. You wanted that hat, those shirts and the jeans."

"And the boots," Duke reminded her. "Lola, will you have dinner with me tonight?"

Her eyes jerked to his. "Tonight? Uh, no...not tonight."

"Too fast, huh? How about tomorrow night?" When she didn't answer, he added, "Let me warn you. I'm going to camp on your doorstep until you say yes."

She tried to laugh. "Really, Mr. Sheridan..."

"Duke."

"All right...Duke. But let *me* warn you that I don't take kindly to pressure."

"Then say yes right now and we'll avoid all that. You name the time and place."

"Thanks for the leeway," she drawled with some sarcasm.

He grinned. "You're welcome. I'm a very fair fellow."

"You know, for some reason I can't quite bring myself to believe that. I think when you see something you want, you don't stop until you get it."

Laughing, he walked a small circle then leaned on the counter. "Guess you understand me."

"Does my understanding present a problem for you?"

"Nope. You see, I understand you, too."

"You only think you do," Lola retorted.

He reached across the counter and flicked the collar of her blouse. "Name the time and place, Lola," he said, his voice low and sensual.

She sucked in a quick breath. Two men were walking through the door. She couldn't stand around and bandy words with Duke Sheridan any longer.

"I can see you're not going to give up," she said quietly. "Make it Friday night. A movie, not dinner. I'm living with Charlie, so you can pick me up at his place at eight."

Duke straightened from the counter with a satisfied expression on his face. "I'll be there. Now, ring up those sales, Lola, my sweet. I've got to get back to the ranch."

Two

The woman occupying room 116 in the redbrick Sundowner Motel checked the Rocky Ford telephone directory, located Fanon, Charles A. and wrote his address, as listed, on the small phone pad provided by the motel. Closing the directory, she set it aside, then stared at the pad. 805 Foxworth Street. Her heart thumped nervously, anxiously. She finally had his exact address. It didn't seem possible, and now that she had gained so much ground, it also seemed a little too easy.

But she had come this far and couldn't start digressing just because one step in her plan had been simple when she'd expected difficult. She realized, in all honesty, that she hadn't really taken the first step yet. Up to now, everything had been a backdrop for what was to come.

Breathing deeply to calm herself, she got up for her purse, left the unit and walked to her car. Right now she would take a look at 805 Foxworth Street. Maybe she'd do more than that today, maybe not. It wasn't that she was lacking in courage, but this was so vastly different from anything else *she'd ever done in her life, with so many emotional ramifications—why wouldn't it demand caution?*

It surprised her, when she found the address, that it wasn't just a house. Foxworth Street had obviously been rezoned from residential to commercial some time ago, because there was both ordinary homes and businesses on each side of the street. Number 805 was a huge old structure that appeared to be a business and a home. It bore a sign over the front porch: Charlie's Place. Driving slowly past, she could see people through the windows. Frowning, she went to the end of the block, turned around and returned to park on the opposite side of the street so she could study the building.

There were other signs, which she thoughtfully read: Best cup of coffee in town. Pastries. Newspapers. Magazines. Her frown went deeper.

People were going in and coming out. Her stomach churned. She hadn't anticipated a business at the address, and it felt like a setback to her goal. After about fifteen minutes of uneasily watching the activity at Charlie's Place, she put the car in gear and drove away.

Charlie had dinner ready when Lola walked in at 6:30. "Something smells very good," she remarked after a cheery hello.

"Homemade vegetable beef soup," Charlie proudly announced.

"Wonderful. Let me get rid of my purse and wash up. I'll be back in a flash."

Just walking through Charlie's big old house brought back memories for Lola. She passed the doors leading to Serena's and Ron's bedrooms, and fondly remembered when the three of them were youngsters and squabbling over the bathroom to wash up for supper. Serena and Ron were Charlie's daughter and son, Lola's cousins, but she loved them as though they were her sister and brother.

Now Ron was in the military, stationed in Germany, involved in something called Special Forces—which meant, to the family's dismay, that whatever he was doing was too secret to talk about. He was married to a beautiful, petite woman named Candace, and they had a young son no one had seen except in snapshots and photographs. The last time Lola had seen Ron in person was at his wedding. He had been stationed in South Carolina at the time, and the whole family had traveled from their various locations to attend the wedding. It was also the last time she had seen Serena, Lola recalled with a sigh. Serena was completely immersed in the study of law at Georgetown University. Mesmerized by Washington, D.C., and politics, she also held a part-time job in a senator's office. In one of her letters, she had humorously described herself as a gofer for a secretary to the senator's main secretary. I'm all but invisible to anyone important, but how I love it, she had written.

Would either Ron or Serena ever return to Rocky Ford? Lola wondered while washing her hands. It would be so great if they could all get together. Charlie would be beside himself if his kids all came home at the same time, if only for a brief visit.

Well, at least she was here, Lola thought, running a brush through her hair. She had mentioned getting her own place when she came home, and Charlie had actually paled. "No, honey, no! I'm so glad you're home, you *have* to stay here. Humor an old man, Lola."

He wasn't an old man, but he was a crafty one, Lola thought with a small laugh. As Duke Sheridan had said, everyone knew Charlie Fanon. What she could have added was that everyone *liked* Charlie Fanon. He was a character, no two ways about it, but thinning hair and slight paunch aside, his infectious smile and kindly nature made him a lovable character.

Anyway, she hadn't looked for an apartment, and she loved living with Charlie again. Her old room was exactly as she had left it, which she planned to do something about one of these days, as high school decor didn't do much for her anymore. But it was so special to know that her own little domain had always been here, even when she'd been on the other side of the globe.

Returning to the large country kitchen, she asked, "Anything I can do, Charlie?"

"Nope. Everything's ready." He placed steaming bowls of soup at her place and his.

They sat down, and Charlie said grace. Smiling at his niece then, he said, "Dive in, but be careful. It's hot."

Lola took a cautious taste. "Hmm, delicious. I knew it would be." She broke off a chunk from the loaf of crusty French bread in a basket between her and Charlie. "So, how'd your day go?" she asked.

"Great, just great," Charlie answered.

Lola smiled. Every day was great to Charlie. He found something good in everyone he met and something good in every day. Most of his customers were old-timers who came in for coffee, doughnuts and gossip. They bought their daily newspaper from Charlie, and their favorite magazines. His business certainly wasn't a high-income venture, but he had started it—renovating the large front parlor of the house—after retiring from the telephone company, where he'd worked as a lineman ever since moving to Montana from California.

"How was your day?" he added after a moment.

"Business was very good, one of the best since I opened the store. Most of it was due to one customer. Charlie, do you know Duke Sheridan?"

Charlie nodded. "I know him. Why? Was he in the store today?"

"He sure was. Uh, Charlie, what do you know about him?"

"About Duke? Well, let me see. He's a successful rancher, hard worker and keeps pretty much to himself."

Lola's eyes widened. "Keeps to himself? Charlie, Duke Sheridan is the biggest flirt I've ever run into."

"Duke is? Never heard that about 'im. Well, I really only know him enough to say hello to. But seems to me that kind of reputation would have spread around town." Charlie cocked an eyebrow and grinned. "Flirted with you, huh? Probably thought you were the cutest little thing he'd ever seen."

"He said something to that effect," Lola said dryly. Her tone of voice changed. "Hasn't he ever been married?"

"Not that I know of. Though I do recall that he and a gal by the name of Tess Hunnicutt were close for quite a spell. Come to think of it, I haven't seen Tess for a long time. Maybe she left town."

Probably over a broken heart, Lola thought with some cynicism. Despite Charlie's good opinion of Duke's reputation, she couldn't stop thinking of the man as a heartbreaker.

"Anyway, he asked me out to dinner. Insisted on it, to be honest. I had customers coming in... Incidentally, Betty had to leave early because her son Brian broke his arm at school. She called from the hospital. Brian's arm was set and casted, and he's doing fine. Betty will be back to work in the morning. But I was very busy, as you can imagine. Duke was pressuring me for a date, and just to get rid of him I finally said yes."

"You could do a whole lot worse than date Duke Sheridan, honey."

"Yes, and maybe I could do a whole lot better." She frowned slightly, remembering the pressure Duke had put on her, making a game of it but pressuring her nonetheless. It had been flattering, yes. He was, after all, one of the best-looking men she'd ever seen. But maybe he was a little too sure of himself, maybe a little too macho. Commitment to any man wasn't at the top of her list of priorities, but someday she hoped to marry and have a family. It was just that Duke didn't quite seem to fit her idea of a life partner.

But then, did she know what kind of man would fit an idea she had never really formulated?

"How old is he, Charlie? Do you know?"

Charlie shook his head. "My guess would be as good as yours. Probably around thirty-five, wouldn't you say?" Charlie's grin flashed. "Good age for a man to settle down."

Lola couldn't help laughing. "One date is not a forerunner to a man settling down, Charlie Fanon."

"No, but every man who ever got married started out with one date, Lola Fanon," Charlie retorted.

"You've already got us married? And I thought Duke was a fast worker," Lola said teasingly. "You've got him beat by a mile."

They laughed together, then Charlie said, "Well, I know some man's gonna sweep you off your feet one of these days, honey, and as I said, you could do worse than Duke Sheridan. When's your date?"

"Friday night. He's going to pick me up at eight."

A twinkle appeared in Charlie's eyes. "Maybe I'll ask him what his intentions are."

"Maybe *I'll* ask about his intentions," Lola said in a quick response.

Charlie grinned. "You'd do it, too, wouldn't you?"

"You bet your sweet bippy I would. One pass and Duke's apt to get an earful."

"That's my girl," Charlie said approvingly. "Keep 'im on the straight and narrow."

"I fully intend to."

That night, lying in bed, Lola wondered how true that statement was. If Duke made a pass, would she really give him what for? He was incredibly attractive, after all, and depending on how the evening went, a good-night kiss might not be at all out of line.

It was a wait-and-see proposition, she decided with a yawn. Turning onto her side, she got comfortable and closed her eyes. It was pleasant to fall asleep thinking of devilish golden brown eyes and a smile that would melt snow during a Montana blizzard.

In his bed at the ranch, Duke stared into the dark and thought about Lola Fanon. He'd gone into her store merely to size it up, not to buy a wardrobe he sure as hell didn't need. That hat, for instance. There were five Stetsons of various colors in his closet, six counting the new one, and he certainly hadn't needed another pair of boots.

But he'd gotten absolutely silly over Lola and started buying things like a love-struck kid, just to keep her talking to him. Damn, she was pretty. Smart, too. And gutsy.

Imagine her traveling all over the world by herself. Had he ever met a more fascinating woman?

"Nope," he mumbled aloud. "Probably never will, either."

He wanted her. The tight, uncomfortable sensation in his gut was unmistakably sexual. But there was more than unfulfilled desire keeping him awake; he liked Lola. He liked her bright mind and self-confidence, the way she moved and held her head so high, the courage with which she obviously faced life. There was only one aspect of her personality that he found a little disturbing, her air of independence.

But hell, a man could get around "independent," couldn't he? Especially when everything else about a woman was damned near perfect?

Heaving a sigh, he forced Lola from his mind to think about the ranch and tomorrow's chores. He had three full-time ranch hands on the payroll, plus an older couple, June and Rufe Hansen. June took care of the house and meals, and Rufe was an all-around handyman, seeing to the grounds, and any repairs to the house, servicing the vehicles and doing any other odd jobs that popped up. The Hansens had been hired by Duke's father, Hugh, about fifteen years ago, so they were sort of like family to Duke. The only family he had, really. They were also the only people who actually lived on the ranch, besides himself, of course. Hugh had built them a little house about a half mile from the main house, giving them and himself privacy. The Sheridan Ranch covered over four thousand acres of prime Montana grazing land, so there was no reason for people to live on top of each other.

Hugh had also built the main house, which Duke now occupied all by his lonesome. He was very different from his father. Hugh had constructed a large house with plenty of bedrooms and bathrooms so he could invite overnight guests to the ranch, which he had done often. Since his death, there'd been no overnight guests in the Sheridan home, not even Tess Hunnicutt, whom Duke had dated for several years.

He frowned in the dark as Tess entered his mind. He had almost married Tess. Rather, she had presumed that conclusion and he had gone along with it until one night when they were together and it struck him that he didn't want to spend the rest of his life with Tess. She was a nonstop talker, which in the early stages of their relationship he had found amusing. But her constant chatter had gradually worn thin. When he realized his loss of feelings for Tess, he had told her in the gentlest way possible that they had no future together. She had stunned him with a scathing fury and a spate of angry words. He'd walked out. About a month later, he'd heard that she had moved to Missoula. Since then there hadn't been anyone important. He had women friends, to be sure, but none who were counting on a wedding ring.

Now there was Lola, who seemed to be head and shoulders above any woman he'd ever met. Time would tell if that was really true, but he knew one thing for certain: he was anxious as hell for Friday night to roll around so he could see her again.

Punching his pillow into a more comfortable configuration, he closed his eyes. He had to get some sleep, since 5:00 a.m. wasn't that far off, and he had a full day of work scheduled for tomorrow.

The lady in the blue sedan was startled to see a young woman leave Charles Fanon's home, get into a red car and drive away. It was 7:45 a.m. She had awakened very early and driven to the Fanon residence and business for another look at the place. The last thing she had expected to see was a young, pretty woman so early in the morning. Obviously the woman had spent the night in the house. Who was she? She seemed too young to be Charles Fanon's wife, but one never knew. Then again, with such a large residence, maybe Charles rented out rooms.

Perplexed, she started her car and followed the red car at a discreet distance. It was driven behind a line of connecting businesses and then parked. When the driver went through one of the back doors of the block-long building, the woman in the blue car slowly drove close enough to the door to see a sign: Deliveries Only. Men's Western Wear.

Okay, so she worked at a men's clothing store. Or maybe the woman owned it. She wanted to get a closer look at the young woman and decided to return later, after the store was open for a while and other customers would be present.

Driving away, she returned to the Sundowner Motel and room 116.

"How is Brian this morning?" Lola asked when Betty arrived at opening time the next morning.

"Brian's fine. The doctor said to keep him quiet for one day, then send him back to school. Mrs. Miller from down the street is at the house with him. She always watches the kids when Tom and I go out, and she was more than happy to stay with Brian today."

"Betty, if Brian's home today, you really didn't have to come in," Lola admonished.

"I promise he's all right," Betty said. "I would never leave one of my kids if they weren't." She then added with an impish smile, "I'm dying to hear what happened with you and Duke Sheridan yesterday."

Lola was preparing the cash register for the day. "What makes you think anything happened?"

"What an innocent expression! You should have been an actress, Lola Fanon."

Lola grinned. "And you should have been a gossip columnist. Okay, I give. There's not that much to tell, anyway. He asked me out. We're seeing a movie together on Friday evening."

"I knew it!" Betty's blue eyes glowed with excitement. "I could tell he fell head over heels the second he saw you."

Lola scoffed. "That's silly. All I am to the flirtatious Mr. Sheridan is a new face."

The first customer of the day walked in, and Betty went to greet him. Finishing her counter work, Lola wondered if she hadn't hit the nail on the head with her comment of merely being a new face to Duke. The idea was oddly discomfiting, but it certainly could be true.

She realized that she really didn't know what to think, and wouldn't know any more about it than she did right now until she spent some time with Duke. What would Friday night bring, disappointment or more intrigue?

Shaking her head over her mental rambling, she walked over to the shirt racks. They had sold quite a few shirts yesterday, and there were gaps on the racks which she closed by rearranging the hangers. A shipment of shirts would arrive today or tomorrow. Good thing she had placed that order when she did, she thought. Without a wide choice of merchandise and sizes, sales would definitely drop off.

It was amazing to her that she was actually making money with her store. Naturally, profit had been her goal when she started this venture, but to think that she was succeeding was extremely gratifying. Apparently she had a head for business, because she was doing everything right. What's more, she loved every aspect of the operation, even to the paperwork.

The bell above the door jangled. Smiling, Lola went to greet the second customer of the morning. From then on, it was a busy day.

Three

As Friday drew nearer, Lola became less concerned about seeing Duke. It was only a date, for heaven's sake, and he was only a person she barely knew. After one evening together she might not want ever to see him again. If that should happen to be the case, it wouldn't bother her to tell him so. Not that she would be cruel or insulting about it. But it took two people to create a relationship, *any* kind of relationship, even ordinary friendship, and if Duke turned out to be unlikable, came on too strong or was boring—unlikely but not impossible—she would let him know that she wasn't interested in furthering their association.

She was glad of one thing, that she hadn't agreed to having dinner with him. A movie was a sensible activity for a first date, much less intimate than a dinner for two in some quiet restaurant. There were several nice restaurants in Rocky Ford, and one especially good place about fifty miles out of town. It was a resort, actually, situated in green mountains with good hiking trails and meandering streams. The rooms and restaurant were expensive, but the Horizon

Resort did a thriving business, both summer and winter, because of its first-class service and excellent food. Charlie had taken her there for dinner during her first week home, proudly showing her what had sprung up while she was away from the area.

The town, too, had done some changing during her extended absence—several housing developments along its outskirts, new businesses, stoplights at intersections that had always been dangerous, and a modernized theater showing the latest movies, to name a few. Growth and progress had reached her hometown, and now she and her store were part of it. She liked that.

When Friday was upon her, however, she became a little uncertain again. All day, in between customers and busy-work, she thought about the date and Duke and how they would get along. She also wondered what to wear for the evening—something casual, of course, but how casual?

She closed at six, as usual, hurried through the after-hours routines—balancing the register, securing the cash in the safe and putting away the sales slips for later attention—and drove home with a knot in her stomach she couldn't dispel with the commonsense arguments she had relied on since agreeing to this date. Okay, she finally admitted, so she was nervous about the evening ahead. No big deal. But when had she ever been nervous about a date? If it had happened before, she couldn't remember it.

Dinner was broiled fish filets and a green salad. She and Charlie discussed the day, as had become a nightly routine, then, together, they did the dishes and straightened the kitchen. Charlie headed for the front part of the house, his business space, to do some sweeping and such, and Lola went to her room to get ready. Time was getting short, and she rushed through a shower and shampoo. After donning fresh lingerie, she grabbed a dress from the closet and put it on. Her hair was easy, just a few minutes with the blow dryer and a styling brush. Makeup took another few minutes, and she was ready with ten minutes to spare.

Good, she thought, stopping to catch her breath. After switching purses, choosing one that matched her dress and flat-heeled shoes, she brought the purse to the kitchen and set it on the table. It was five minutes to eight.

Hearing a vehicle pulling into the driveway, she peeked out the window and saw a black four-wheeler. It was a large expensive model with four doors, and as clean and shiny as a freshly polished mirror. Duke got out. Lola's breath caught in her throat. He was wearing blue-gray Western pants and shirt, and black boots, appearing so handsome in the day's waning light that she felt choked just looking at him.

"Whoa," she mumbled to herself, not particularly thrilled that the mere sight of a man would cause her so much turmoil.

She let him knock twice on the kitchen door, which really had become the front door ever since Charlie had turned the front of the house into a business. Finally, calmly, she walked to the door and opened it.

"Hello," she said with a smile.

"Hello." Duke's gaze glided over her pretty, dusky rose dress and slippers, then up to her face. She was every bit as appealing as he remembered, even more so in that dress.

"I'm ready," Lola said, stepping away from the door to pick up her purse.

"We've got a few minutes before the movie starts. I'd like to say hello to Charlie, if it's all right with you."

"Well, yes, of course. He's in the front." Leading the way, she called, "Charlie?"

They entered the big room with its tables and chairs, display shelves containing books and magazines, and its wonderful smell of rich coffee beans. Charlie set aside his broom.

Duke slipped around Lola and offered his hand. "Hello, Charlie."

"Duke." They shook hands.

"Been awhile since I've been in here," Duke said with a glance around. "Nice place."

"It'll never make me a rich man, but it gives me something to do," Charlie said with a small chuckle. "Never could abide sitting around and doing nothing."

"We've got that in common," Duke said. "I've never figured out if that kind of drive is a curse or a blessing, though. Have you?"

Charlie rubbed his jaw. "Can't say that I have. Most of my customers are older folks, and a goodly percent of them are completely content with retirement. Me, now, I was going a little stir crazy after retirement till I hit on the idea of opening this place."

"Well, you've done a good job with it." Duke glanced at his watch. "Guess we'd better be going if we're going to see the start of the movie. Nice talking to you, Charlie."

"Nice of you to say hello, Duke. Stop in anytime."

Knowing her uncle so well, Lola caught the respect in his voice and demeanor. Maybe it was only good manners for Duke to say hello to Charlie, but she couldn't help suspecting an ulterior motive. Like, maybe, his playing up to her uncle would influence her opinion of him?

They left by the kitchen door and walked to Duke's vehicle, where he opened the front passenger door for her to get in.

"Thank you." Her words were rather clipped and unfriendly. Even she noticed it. But she wasn't going to be railroaded into anything by Duke, who already seemed to have gained the upper hand simply by saying a few words to Charlie. She thought about those few minutes with the three of them together while Duke strode to the driver's door. Charlie's respect had been so obvious—to her, anyway—and since Charlie Fanon, to her knowledge, had never been impressed by material possessions, his respect had to have been focused strictly on Duke himself. It seemed a little odd when Charlie had told her that he knew Duke only well enough to say hello to.

Duke got in and started the motor. Laying his arm along the top of the seat, he turned and used the rear window to back out of the driveway. On the street, he pointed the vehicle in the direction of the movie theater and got under way.

Setting her purse on the seat between them, Lola pulled down her seat belt and fastened it. Duke sent her a teasing glance. "Worried about my running into something?"

She didn't think seat belts were anything to laugh about. "If my parents had been wearing seat belts, they might not have been killed in that car accident," she said evenly, staring straight ahead while she spoke.

There was a moment of silence from Duke, then he said a subdued "Sorry" and hooked his own seat belt. She made no comment.

Duke cleared his throat. "Um...nice evening." For some reason they weren't off to a great start.

"Yes, it is," Lola agreed. "It's supposed to rain this weekend, though."

"Yes, I heard the weather report on the news. Had the radio on in my bedroom while I was getting ready. It's to be expected, though. In fact, we've had a three-week dry spell, a little out of the ordinary for spring in these parts."

"We've had a lovely spring. I don't mind rain, as long as it doesn't drag on for weeks."

The theater came into view. Lola stared. "Good Lord, what's going on there tonight?" There were dozens of teenagers milling around in front of the theater.

Duke frowned. "I have no idea. Wait a minute." He'd noticed the marquee. "That's not the movie that was on the marquee yesterday."

"No, it's not." In bold letters on the marquee, the title of a prehistoric monster movie was spelled out. "I don't want to see that."

"Neither do I. In fact, I saw it years ago. It's a kids' movie. I'm going to park and talk to someone." After pulling to the curb, he asked, "Want to wait here or come with me?"

"I'll wait here."

The young people on the sidewalk were talking, laughing and cutting up as teenagers do, and Lola found herself smiling with old memories of herself at that age. Everything had seemed funny during those years, and she and her friends had giggled their way through high school. Until the middle of her junior year, she remembered, when suddenly—so it seemed—she grew up and began thinking seriously of the future.

She was still deep in her own past when she spotted Bud Hawkins in the crowd. Bud was one of the teenagers who worked part-time in the store. Rolling down the window, she called, "Bud?"

He glanced over, saw her and ambled to the car. Bending down, he peered through the window. "Hi, Miss Fanon."

"Hi, Bud. What's going on here tonight?"

"They started showing special movies a couple of Friday nights a month to get the kids off the streets," Bud said matter of factly. "You haven't heard about it?"

"No, I haven't."

"Well, there's not much for kids to do in Rocky Ford, so I guess a bunch of people got together and came up with this idea. Mr. Jules, the theater owner, went along with it, so here we are. Guess it's working. It's someplace to go, anyway. The Eagles Lodge holds dances when there isn't something going on at school, too. Between the high school, Mr. Jules and the Eagles, there's always somewhere to go on Friday nights now."

"Sounds terrific, Bud." Lola bit her lip for a moment. She had been remiss about getting involved in town politics and problems. As a business owner, she really should join the Chamber of Commerce and the other organizations that worked for the betterment of the community.

"Anyone can go see the movie, though," Bud continued. "It's not strictly confined to kids, but the tickets are half price to anyone under eighteen, and Mr. Jules sells the popcorn and sodas at a lower price than he usually does."

"Sounds to me like Mr. Jules is doing his part to help the young people of Rocky Ford."

"Guess so." Bud grinned. "But so are you, Miss Fanon. My job in your store is the best thing that's ever happened to me."

"That's good to hear, Bud. I hadn't realized..." Duke was suddenly at the window, too. "Oh, Bud, do you know Mr. Sheridan?"

Bud stood up. "Hi, Duke."

"Hello, Bud. How's it going?"

"Pretty well."

"How's your dad?"

"Doing all right. The doc says he can go back to work in about two more weeks."

"That's great."

"Yeah, it is. Well, everyone's going in. Guess I'd better join the troops. See ya." He dipped his head to speak to Lola. "See ya next week, Miss Fanon."

Lola nodded. "On Monday afternoon. Bye, Bud."

Duke walked around the car and got in. "You got the scoop from Bud, I'll bet."

"Yes, he explained. Sounds like the whole town is cooperating to give the young people sensible entertainment. When I was in high school, Friday night was date night and most of the time there wasn't anything to do."

"Same here." Duke was looking at her. "So, the kids have something to do and we don't. Any suggestions?"

There were the taverns, of course. Some of them provided live music on weekends for their patrons, but Lola wasn't particularly fond of saloons.

She heaved a sigh. "Not really."

"Then I have one. Do you remember the Lockland Grange? It's been there for a hundred years, so you might remember it. If you ever went there, that is."

"I do remember it. Why?"

"There's a dance there tonight."

A dance at the Lockland Grange. Pleasant memories bombarded Lola. "Do they still play the old-time music?"

"Piano, guitar and fiddle," Duke confirmed. "Other than an occasional coat of paint, the Grange never changes."

Lockland Grange was thirty miles away, in a rural community whose inhabitants farmed rather than ranched. Lola smiled nostalgically. "When we were teenagers, Charlie took us kids to two or three of those dances. Gosh, that seems like a long time ago." Thinking of her chat with Bud, she looked at Duke. "Don't the kids go out there anymore?"

"Not much. Probably because of the music. They've got their own style of music, Lola, much more so than our generation did."

Lola nodded. "You're probably right, but I remember liking all kinds of music."

A moment of silence ensued. Duke gave her a look. "Well, how about it? Want to go?"

She thought for a second. Did she want to dance with Duke? On the other hand, the Grange was not a place of low lights and romantic music. The band played polkas and waltzes and two-steps. Even some old-time schottisches. And she had learned the Virginia reel out there many years ago. If they still played those old songs and rhythms, she could dance with anyone without worrying about intimacy.

"Yes," she said with conviction. "It sounds like fun."

"Great." Duke got the car moving.

"Did something happen to Bud's father?" Lola asked when they were on their way. The boy hadn't mentioned his father to her.

"Jake Hawkins works for a building contractor. He fell from a roof rafter and broke both legs about two months back. I was glad to hear Bud say he's doing all right."

Lola turned her head to look at Duke. "You know everyone in the area, don't you?"

"Just about." Duke took his eyes from the road to return her look. "Don't you? You grew up here, too."

"Yes, but I've been gone for so long . . . since high school graduation, really. After that it was college, then—"

"Where'd you go to college?" Duke asked.

"I started in Bozeman, then transferred to Tempe, Arizona."

"Wanderlust had already set in?"

"I think I was born with wanderlust," Lola said with a small laugh.

"But you came home. Where's all that wanderlust now?"

"Gone. I guess I used it up."

"Are you as sure of that as you sound?"

"Positive. I'm right where I want to be, where I plan to stay."

"So there really is no place like home?"

"Exactly," Lola murmured. "For me, anyway." It had happened rather suddenly, she recalled. One day she was content living thousands of miles from Montana and home, and the next day she wasn't. It had taken some time for the loneliness to really settle in, but when it did, she sold everything she possessed except for her clothes and bought a plane ticket.

"Why did you go into business?" Duke asked.

"Why?" she echoed. "That's a strange question. I wanted something to do, of course."

"But you could have gotten a job. Why take on the headaches of operating a business?"

She turned in the seat, enough to give him a good long look. "You're just full of questions, aren't you?"

His eyes left the road to slide in her direction. "I don't know any way to get answers other than to ask questions, do you?"

"And you're looking for answers? Why, Duke?"

"Only because I'm interested, Lola, very interested. I haven't told you how beautiful you look in that dress, but you do. You're an especially beautiful woman in any case, but the color of that dress is perfect for you."

"That's what the saleslady said when I tried it on in a little backstreet shop in Paris. She was trying to sell me the dress, Duke. What are you trying to sell me?"

He sent her a grin. "You have a suspicious nature, sweetheart."

She lifted her chin. "You're flirting again, like you did the day you came into the store. Do you know something, Duke? You're more than one person."

"I'm what?" he asked with a laugh.

"Who were you with Charlie and Bud? You were very different with them than you are with me."

"Well, I would hope so," he said with a snort of laughter. "I have absolutely no desire to date either one of them."

She put on a saccharine smile. "Very funny."

"If I'm so funny, how come you're not laughing?"

"I was being sarcastic. As if you didn't know."

Duke made a right turn from the highway onto another road. "You're fighting this, aren't you?"

"Fighting what?"

"What's happening between us. I have to ask myself why you'd do that. You see, with you being the self-confident, independent woman you are, I don't think you'd be in this car with me right now if you'd rather be somewhere else. Which leads me to believe that you like me. Stop me if I'm wrong," he said, sending her a quick glance, before asking point-blank, "*do* you like me?"

She gave an incredulous laugh. "We barely know each other. What on earth are you hoping I'll say?"

"Just the truth, honey. Just the plain old truth."

"The unvarnished truth, Duke Sheridan, is that you're making me very uncomfortable."

"Ah, a clue to your inner feelings."

"Clue, my left foot! I wish you'd stop trying to figure me out."

"Aren't you trying to figure me out?"

"Absolutely not. I *thought* we were going to see a movie. Going to a movie with a man doesn't call for an analysis of his psyche. At least I never thought it did."

"I have a totally different opinion on that subject," Duke said calmly. "When a man and woman meet for the first time and the air all but sizzles around them, I think they start delving into each other's personality right from the get-go."

She arched an eyebrow. "Oh, really?" But she didn't refute his remark about "sizzling air," though it was certainly an exaggeration of their first meeting. Still, denying that she had felt something uniquely exciting that day would be a lie, and she suspected that he would be only too willing to debate the point. It was a discussion she preferred avoiding, even though she usually spoke her mind without wondering if she should. A disturbing thought came to her. If Duke was a different person with her, so was she with him. What should she make of that?

"Almost there," Duke remarked, making another turn. "Getting back to personalities—"

She cut in, "Let's not."

"Do you usually avoid controversial conversations?"

"No, I do not. But I think you're making far too much of a first date."

Duke took one hand from the wheel and snapped his fingers. "I got it now. You're more willing to talk about meaningful relationships on a *second* date."

Giving him a startled look, she saw the humorous waggling of his eyebrows in the dash lights.

"You are having far too good a time at my expense," she accused.

He laughed. "I am having a good time, honey. But that's only because I'm with you. You're not mad at me for teasing you a little, are you?"

He was too damned cute, but her annoyance melted away until she gave a small laugh. "No, I'm not mad at you."

"That's good. It's hard dancing with someone who's mad at you."

"I'm sure you've had the experience," she said dryly.

"There's another topic you probably won't talk about on a first date."

She looked at him quizzically. "What topic?"

"Experience. I'm sure you must have met some interesting people during your travels."

"Yes, of course."

Duke cleared his throat. "Interesting men?"

She tilted her head to see him. "By any chance, are you asking about my experience with men?"

"Well, I am curious."

"Would you like me to tell you what you can do with your curiosity, Mr. Sheridan?" she asked sweetly.

"Uh, probably not." He chuckled after a moment. "We sure do get along, don't we?"

Lola merely shook her head in amazement, though in truth she had been enjoying their repartee. Duke was fun to be with, flagrantly nosy but fun. Scratch "boring," she thought, recalling her thoughts about what kind of evening they might have together.

"There's the Grange," Duke announced.

Lola looked ahead and saw the lights of the old building. Dozens of cars and pickup trucks were parked around the place.

"Looks like a good turnout," she remarked.

Duke pulled into the parking lot and found an empty space. He turned off the ignition. The second the motor was silent, they could hear music coming from the building. Lola smiled: it was the same type of old-time music she remembered. She reached for the door handle to get out, and felt Duke's hand on her arm.

She turned to look at him. "What?"

"If you'll wait a minute, I'll be a gentleman and open your door for you."

She laughed. "That's not necessary. I'm perfectly capable of opening the door for myself."

"Lola, sit," he said firmly, and bounded from the car to hurry around the front of his car.

"You silly man," she whispered. But there was something alive and happy within her. She could have easily and honestly given Duke an answer to his question *Do you like me?* She did like him. Very much.

But it was that very affection that had her guard up. Never before had she so quickly developed positive feelings for a man. To her way of thinking, that in itself was reason enough to keep their relationship in the sane and sensible category, especially when she suspected that, given an opening, Duke would make a move on her with the impact of a speeding bullet.

He opened her door. She looked at the hand he extended in invitation for a moment before taking it and heard Duke laugh softly.

Okay, maybe she was being a little too cautious. Gingerly she placed her hand in his and got out of the car. The next thing she knew she was pressed against Duke, thigh to thigh, chest to chest. Startled, she lifted her chin to look into his eyes. His arms were around her, holding her firmly in place.

"Don't do this, Duke," she said in a voice that was suddenly husky with rampaging emotions.

"You don't kiss on a first date?" There was a teasing quality to his voice, even though his eyes were dark and sober. "I want to kiss you, Lola," he whispered. "I've hardly thought of anything else since we met."

She saw his head slowly coming down. Her own heartbeat was nearly choking her.

But she wasn't ready for this move. Placing her hands on his chest, she shoved hard and took a backward step at the same time.

"Cool it, sport," she mumbled thickly. "I won't be rushed."

Duke stared at her, then laughed. "Guess I forgot that. Come on, let's go in."

Lola frowned as they wound through vehicles to reach the Grange. He'd taken rejection well. This time. What concerned her was that the next time he made a pass—and she had no doubt that he would try again—she might not say no.

She could get in very deep, very fast with Duke Sheridan. A heavy but silent sigh lifted her shoulders. After little more than an hour together, things were already getting complicated.

Was she falling for Duke? Maybe she was, though an even more disturbing question was what he really thought of her. If he was looking for nothing more than sex, he was barking up the wrong tree.

But how would she know? More than one woman had fallen for a charming, handsome man, given him everything including her heart, and then been dropped like a hot potato when another challenging woman appeared on the scene.

Why did she suspect Duke of being that type of guy? No one had said anything to lead her to believe that about him. It was more of a gut instinct than anything else.

A final thought just before they reached the door of the Grange weakened her knees. Was it possible that she was merely devising arguments against falling in love and would do the same with any man who expressed a serious interest in her?

Four

─────

A blue sedan was parked in the dark shadow of a huge cottonwood tree, directly across the street from Charlie's Place. The woman inside the car sat rigid as a rock, staring intently at the lighted windows of the Fanon residence. A man was in and out of sight, appearing to be doing some cleaning. She couldn't see his features clearly and wished she had binoculars with her. Even the vague picture he presented, however, made her heart beat faster. *Charles Albert Fanon.* Instinctively she knew it was him. This was her chance. She should take it . . . now!

Her muscles became even stiffer than they'd been and her thoughts began stumbling over one another. Panic rose in her throat, and it took several minutes to even partially calm herself.

She knew the name of the dark-haired young woman living with Charles . . . Lola Fanon. She had visited the Men's Western Wear store, going in when the two female clerks were busy with customers. Browsing, she had managed to get close enough to read Lola's courtesy tag on her blouse.

The Fanon name had dealt her a blow. Who was she to Charles? The rent-a-room theory was out; Lola Fanon had to be closely related, probably a daughter.

Then, earlier tonight, she had seen Lola leave with a man in a black vehicle. Ever since, she had been watching Charles through the windows of his house and business.

She inhaled a deep breath, waiting for the courage to climb the stairs to the front porch, to go through that door, to do what she had come to Montana and Rocky Ford to do.

"Oh, God," she moaned. She could never leave town until she accomplished her goal, and here was a perfect opportunity to do so. He was all alone in that big house. Why couldn't she get out of this car?

Her mind raced, looking for answers. Was it because she still didn't know enough about Charles Fanon? Enough about Lola? Maybe he had more children than Lola. If so, where were they? Where was his wife?

There were too many questions confusing her. She could not do it tonight.

The decision was relieving. Her body lost some of its tension.

When the lights went out in the front part of the house, she started the car and slowly drove away.

The second Duke paid for their admittance to the Lockland Grange, he pulled Lola onto the dance floor. Surprised, she laughed but fell into the steps of the waltz being played by the people making music on a piano, guitar and fiddle.

She glanced around in amazement while they danced. "It's exactly the same."

"Told you it was," Duke said.

"Yes, but after so many years I expected *some* change. The ladies still have their tables of snacks and drinks to sell along that west wall, and the piano is in the exact spot it always was."

"Some things never change," Duke said.

"Very few."

"Have you noticed changes in the area since you returned?"

"Lots of them."

"And you don't like change?"

"To the contrary, I've always enjoyed change. Actively sought it, to be honest. Until recently," she said. "I'm talking about personal change now," she added after a moment.

"So you were a changeable woman and now you're not?"

She nodded. "Something like that."

"How'd that happen?"

Good question, she thought, and gave a small shrug in response. "The band members can't possibly be the same people who were here when I was a teenager, but they seem the same," she said, instead of replying to Duke's question.

A man said, "Hey, Duke," as he and his partner danced by. Duke returned the greeting, and then said hello to another couple.

"This is not the place to come if one wants privacy," he said to Lola with a laugh.

She smiled sweetly. "But one doesn't really want privacy, does one?"

"One would thoroughly enjoy privacy, but by your standards, one cannot make a unilateral decision on a first date." He stared into her eyes until her smile weakened and faded, and her heart was pounding. Then he spoke only loud enough so she would be the sole recipient of his words. "I'm looking forward to our second date."

It was then that she realized how hard she'd been working to keep from acknowledging how incredible it was being in his arms, dancing with him, breathing in his scent. He wasn't holding her too close, but it wasn't possible to dance without their bodies brushing together now and then. He was so much taller than she was, and she had to tilt her head to see his face.

It struck her then: he was a possessive man. He was talking about a second date as though it were a given. As though she had nothing to say about it.

"You're very sure of yourself, aren't you?" she said, also speaking quietly. "We're in the middle of a first date and you're thinking about the next one. Duke, don't ever make the mistake of taking me for granted. I'm not at all sure there's going to be a second date."

His gaze held hers, and his arms tightened around her, just enough to bring her a little nearer. "There will be," he whispered. "Count on it."

She jerked back a step, putting space between them. At the same time the song ended and people began moving around, some couples waiting for the next dance and chatting with their neighbors, some leaving the floor.

Duke's confidence made Lola nervous. She took another step back from him and couldn't quite look him in the eye. "I'm going to get something to drink," she said, and immediately started for the west side of the building.

Following, Duke studied her rigid posture through narrowed, thoughtful eyes. She was the most exciting, fascinating woman he'd ever known, but she was also the most stubborn and independent. Instead of saying she was thirsty and giving him the chance to offer her a soda or something, she had announced almost belligerently that she was going to get a drink and left to do it. If he hadn't followed, he would be standing on the dance floor by himself, and apparently she just hadn't given a damn. He never would have done that to her, or to any woman, for that matter, and because of her disregard for his feelings, there was a small surge of anger in his system to contend with.

She ordered ice tea from the lady behind the drink table, opened her purse and paid for it. Duke seethed silently, then ordered himself a lemonade. A man he knew came up, and they started talking. Lola moved away a little and sipped her tea, her gaze roving over the crowd. Spotting a few people *she* knew, she waved and smiled.

The music began again, a two-step. Duke walked over to her. Resentment for her independence made his voice sarcastic. "If you would have waited a minute, you could have paid for my drink, too."

Her head jerked around. "Oh, please. I suspected it all along, but you have just proven how superior you feel to women."

"That's ridiculous. I don't feel one bit superior to you or any other woman. But when I take a woman out for an evening, I expect to foot the bill."

Lola faced the dance floor with a disgusted grimace. "This tea cost seventy-five cents. Reimburse me, if that's what it takes to appease your obviously wounded pride."

"It's not the money, damn it. It . . . it's propriety."

She turned to look at the stubborn jutting of his chin, and all of a sudden realized how rude she had been. Leaving a man on the dance floor was something she had never done in her life. What on earth was wrong with her? And ordering and paying for her drink without asking if he wanted one had been rude, as well. The word *propriety* sounded strange coming out of his mouth, but it really did fit the situation.

"I'm sorry," she said, though without meekness or timidity. She was not a meek or timid woman and never would be, not even when offering an apology.

Duke looked at her for a moment, then slowly shook his head. "You're one tough cookie, aren't you?"

"If you mean that I'm accustomed to taking care of myself, yes."

"And no man is ever going to tell you what to do, is he?"

She gave him a hard look. "Do you permit women to tell you what to do?"

"That's different. I'm a man."

"A superior being, right?"

"Dammit, Lola . . ."

"That's it," she said, moving to the table to set down her glass. He still made her nervous and they didn't speak the same language. There was no point in prolonging the evening. As Duke was right behind her she didn't have to raise her voice to add, "I'd like to leave now." She could see the tightening of his lips. He was getting angry and so was she.

"We just got here," he growled.

"Stay if you like. You have a lot of friends here. I'm sure you could have a good time without my company. I'll wait in the car." She started for the door.

Cursing under his breath, Duke placed his glass on the table and took off after her. Outside she picked up speed and hurried to the car, all but feeling his angry breath on the back of her neck and determined to stay ahead of him.

She reached for the door handle. He took her arm and whirled her around to face him.

"What the hell's going on?" he asked through clenched teeth.

"Hold it right there, buster," she said, jerking her arm free. "I don't know what kind of women you're used to dating, but *this* woman will not be manhandled!"

"Why are you ruining the evening?"

"Me?" Her expression conveyed astonishment. "From where I stand, you're the one doing the ruining."

"How? By trying to pay for your drink? Who left whom looking like an idiot on the dance floor?"

"I already apologized for that," she said sharply, then took a calming breath. "Look, this was obviously a mistake. I can't pretend to be the kind of woman you seem to prefer."

"Which is? Since you're so brilliant and all-seeing, why don't you tell me what kind of woman I prefer."

Her eyes narrowed menacingly. "Are you trying to pick a fight?"

"Are you?" he shot back.

Disgusted again, she turned away. "This is the most stupid conversation I've ever been a part of." She glared openly at him. "Are you going to drive me back to town?"

"Gladly!" he shouted. "And I wouldn't dream of insulting you again by trying to open the car door for you. Get in!"

She almost didn't. Fuming, she stood there until he was behind the wheel. Of all the arrogant, chauvinistic know-it-alls, Duke Sheridan was the worst!

But she was thirty miles from town and common sense prevailed. She got in the car, slamming the door behind her.

Duke started the motor with a roar that conveyed utter fury on his part, and she hastily latched her seat belt, certain that he was going to drive ludicrously fast and recklessly because he was in a snit.

He surprised her by driving at a sensible speed, no differently than he had on the trip out to the Grange. After a few miles she began to relax. Glancing at Duke, she saw him staring straight ahead, his profile granite hard.

She rolled her eyes. "Give it a rest, Duke. I'm big enough to admit tonight was a mistake. You should be able to do the same."

"You were determined to make it a mistake, from the minute I picked you up tonight."

"That's the silliest thing I've ever heard," she scoffed. "Why would I deliberately sabotage a simple date?"

"Because it isn't simple for either of us."

Her head came around slowly. "What's that supposed to mean?"

"It means there's something powerful between us, and none of your displays of petulant independence is going to destroy it." He paused briefly before stating flatly, "You're afraid to let yourself like me."

Lola's jaw dropped. "Afraid! How damned conceited can one man be? Listen, sport, I am not now nor ever will be afraid of you and...and what you apparently consider to be killer charm."

"You're the one with the charm, lady. You reeled me in like a fish on a line."

"I did no such thing! Your imagination is working overtime. But then, with your ego you would naturally have to come up with a reason to blame me because we don't get along. It couldn't possibly be the perfect Duke Sheridan's fault."

"Be as sarcastic as you please. Facts are facts."

"As you see them. There are two sides to every story, and my side..."

"Is scared spitless. What's the matter, Lola? Haven't you ever met a man before who knocked you for a loop?"

She sucked in a startled breath. "That is without a doubt the most self-centered, egotistical thing any man has ever said to me. Do you really believe you're irresistible?"

"What I believe is that we liked each other the moment we met. What I believe is that you got to thinking about it and decided you could be getting too close to the real thing with me, and the real thing scares the hell out of you. You don't want any serious intruders on your little world, and—"

"Just stop right there! First of all, my world is not little. I've seen a hell of a lot more of the world than you have, and I chose—*chose*—to come back to Montana and make a life for myself here."

"Yeah, and you're a mature, all grown-up girl, aren't you? How come you're living with Charlie if you're so self-sufficient and indomitable?"

"I *like* living with Charlie, you . . . you jerk! And I don't have to explain myself or anything I do to you." Duke suddenly wheeled the car into a wide, open area at the side of the road. "What're you doing?"

"This," he growled, and slid across the seat. Before she could do more than gasp, he was holding her face in his hands and kissing her lips. The fight drained out of her as quickly as air leaves a pricked balloon. His size and scent were overwhelming, and his mouth on hers was like no other kiss she had ever received. An ache in the pit of her stomach was instantaneous, and in the space of two seconds she was kissing him back.

Duke unhooked her seat belt and put his arms around her. Hers went up around his neck. There was barely a breath between the first kiss and the second. That one was rough and hungry, and Lola felt herself sinking into it with a feverish desire she had no wish to control. Her fingers wound through his hair. His tongue darted in and out of her mouth.

A moan built in her throat. Passion was no stranger; there had been a few memorable men in her past.

But none to compare with Duke. The strength of his body was unquestionable; the strength of his desire was overpowering and influencing her own.

She felt his hand on the bodice of her dress, moving from breast to breast. And each kiss he gave her was hotter than the one before. He was breathing hard, and so was she.

His hand slithered under her skirt, sliding up her thighs. Tearing her mouth from his, barely able to speak, she whispered hoarsely, "Don't...don't." Bringing her own hand down, she took hold of his.

"Lola...sweetheart...don't stop me," he whispered raggedly. "I want you so much."

She wanted him, too, but they were in a public place. Cars were passing by. What if someone she knew caught sight of her in Duke's arms, parked alongside of the road?

"We can't do this here." She was as breathless as if she had just run a mile.

Dipping his head, he nuzzled her throat. "Where, then?"

"Where?" she echoed numbly, trying hard to think clearly, though her mind felt fuzzy and addled. Were they actually talking about finding a place to make love? Was she really going to make love with a man she hardly knew? Every cell in her body was urging her to do it, to go somewhere with him where they could finish what had been started with a kiss she hadn't been at all prepared for.

She was gripping his hand through the fabric of her skirt. If she let go of it, she knew where it would end up. An aching desire battled with common sense. His breath was hot on her skin, his mouth moving on her throat. She wanted this man more than she'd ever wanted anything.

But it was too soon...too fast.

"Give...give me some breathing room," she stammered. "I need to think."

Duke lifted his head to peer at her face. "Don't think, honey. Thinking will ruin everything."

But she was already thinking. "You're moving too fast. Please take me home."

"Lola," he groaned, burying his face in her throat again. "Don't do this. We need each other."

It was true. She did need him, with a desperation she had never before experienced. But that was what scared her, that he could make her body ache and throb with just a few kisses, and that he could make her want to forget everything else but him. How could he have so much power over her senses?

She inhaled a deep, shaky breath. "Duke, I really do want to go home."

He tried to kiss her again, and she moved her head so his lips fell on her cheek. She knew what he was hoping for, to kiss and caress her into submission. It could work, too, if she allowed any more intimacy.

"Don't," she said huskily. "No more, Duke."

He, too, inhaled deeply. But he sat up straighter. "All right, no more for tonight," he said. "Will you go out with me tomorrow night?"

She hastened to pull her skirt down over her knees. "I...I don't know."

"You're shaken up."

She looked at him. "Yes, I am. I didn't expect..."

"You should have. It's been between us from the moment we met." He took her hand. "Lola, it's not going to go away. I'm going to lie in my bed tonight and think of you, and you're going to lie in your bed and think of me. We're not kids. We should be in the same bed."

"Don't say that!"

"Why not? Dammit, tell me why not."

"Because...because we only met a few days ago," she blurted, the only answer she'd been able to piece together from the confusion in her brain.

He was silent a few moments, staring at her. "You think time will make a difference? I'm going to want you just as much next week."

Lola's stomach churned. He could win this argument, and she didn't dare let that happen. Regardless of the discomfort in her own body, all caused by him, they *didn't* know each other well enough to share the same bed. This was still a first date, whether Duke preferred to ignore that fact or not.

"Is that your line with every woman?" she asked, knowing full well the question would anger him. But she had to stop his persuasive tactics. Maybe anger would cool his ardor.

"Are 'lines' what you're accustomed to hearing from men?" He spoke tensely, but not angrily. "If so, you've been hanging out with the wrong crowd."

"I haven't been *hanging* out with anyone," she said sharply, feeling defensive about her personal life, or rather, the lack thereof. "For your information, I've been too busy getting the store on track to waste time on personal pursuits."

"In other words, you haven't done any dating since you came home. If that's the case, how come you said yes to me?"

"Because you pressured me into it!"

"I doubt very much that anyone, man or woman, could pressure you into anything you didn't want." Duke slid back across the seat. Checking the highway for oncoming traffic, he pulled out of the wayside clearing and onto the road.

"You know," he said after a minute, "your choice of words is very interesting. Do you really think the pursuit of personal pleasure is a waste of time?"

"What?" she asked with a startled frown.

"You said that you've been too busy with the store to waste time on personal pursuits. Should I take that to mean the only thing you do is work?"

"Of course it's not the only thing I do! Why do you twist everything I say to suit your obviously one-track mind?" she all but shrieked.

"You don't need to yell. I'm not deaf. And I don't have a one-track mind." He thought a moment. "Except with you. Where you're concerned, maybe I do have a one-track mind," he admitted.

"Yes, and we both know what rut it's in, don't we?" she said with heavy sarcasm.

He gave a brief, cynical laugh. "If you think I'm going to apologize for liking and wanting you, think again. At least I'm honest about it. You're as hot for me as I am for you, only you're too damned cowardly to admit it. To do something about it," he added after a second.

"What you call cowardly, I call sensible," she retorted. "Your opinion of my morals is insulting. Do you think I fall into bed with every man who smiles at me?"

"We've done a little more than smile at each other," Duke said dryly. "If we'd been in a more, uh, propitious setting, nothing would have stopped us. And you know it, too."

"And that's your plan, to get me in a 'more, uh, propitious setting,'" she said, mimicking his hesitation over the word *propitious*.

He surprised her by laughing. Apparently, whatever anger he'd felt a short time ago had vanished. In fact, she was beginning to think that he enjoyed arguing with her.

"Lola, Lola," he drawled lazily. "You have a very suspicious nature."

"You bet I do," she snapped. He might not be angry now, but she was red hot and seething inside.

"My feelings for you are going deeper by the minute," he said, flashing her a smile that she saw as smug.

Her anger increased tenfold. How dare he be smug with her? Gritting her teeth, she said the most insulting thing she could think of. "Your only feelings for me are below your belt, so don't try to con me, Duke."

"You're angry."

"I'm not only angry, I don't like you. There's the answer to your question. Are you happy now? You finally dragged it out of me."

He chuckled. "I don't think you're a liar, so what you're doing is trying to con both of us. You like me, Lola, you like me a lot. When a woman kisses back the way you did, she doesn't dislike the man who's holding her."

Damn his black soul, he was right. "It won't be repeated, believe me," she said in a searing tone.

"Sure it will."

"It will not!" she shrieked. It took every ounce of willpower she possessed to calm herself. "I'm not going to say another word to you. You're too conceited to be believed, so this... this ridiculous discussion is over. Just drive and leave me alone."

To her surprise he did exactly that. After awhile the lights of town were a welcome sight. She released a tension-laden breath. If she never saw Duke Sheridan again, it would be too soon.

He drove directly to Charlie's Place and pulled into the driveway. Leaving the motor running, he turned in the seat to look at Lola.

"Thank you for a wonderful evening," he said with laughter lurking in his voice. "I can't remember when I've had a better time."

"You . . . you snake! Thanks for nothing!" she snapped, and opened her door.

Getting out, she heard him say, "I'll be calling."

She stopped to glare a moment, then spun and marched to the house. She couldn't be sure, but she thought she heard him laughing again.

Five

————

Lola couldn't remember if she had ever put in a worse night—rolling and tossing, throwing her covers around, falling into a troubled sleep only to wake up again and again. The whole miserable night was Duke's fault, she thought irritably when her alarm went off and she reached for it with mayhem in mind. Instead of murdering the clock, though, she pushed the Off button and crawled grumpily out of bed. Saturdays were always busy at the store, and she needed to get there early today to do some computer work before opening the doors.

After a shower she at least felt alive. Charlie was always up before daybreak, and there was a small pot of coffee in the kitchen for her, although he was already doing business in the front of the house. He opened early—6:00 a.m.—as many of his customers were retired people who got up with the birds and came to his place for their morning coffee and newspaper. Then they dribbled in throughout the day, mostly to see Charlie. Longtime residents of Rocky Ford, Charlie's patrons and friends knew everything going on in town and delighted in passing on gossip and discussing local politics, sometimes getting into heated debates when there were opposing viewpoints among them. Charlie's Place had become a gathering spot, and little that occurred in the area slipped past the regulars without comment.

Another thing Charlie had done was put in several sets of tables and chairs for card players, and nearly every afternoon there were folks in his place playing pinochle, gin rummy or bridge.

Pouring herself a cup of coffee from the kitchen pot, Lola could hear voices and laughter in the front. She smiled: it sounded as if Charlie and his cronies were telling jokes. Her smile faded quickly. Some mornings she went in to say hello and help herself to one of the fresh donuts, bagels or Danish that Charlie had delivered from the town's best bakery every day. This morning she didn't feel like chatting and kidding around with anyone, so she made herself a piece of toast and ate it standing at a window looking out at the gray, overcast sky. From the dark clouds overhead, it appeared rain was imminent.

Pouring the remaining coffee in the pot into a thermos to take with her, Lola left the house. After parking her car in her usual spot behind her store, she unlocked the heavy utility door and went in.

She was working with the inventory control program in her computer when she sat back. As ridiculous and impossible as it was, Duke's face seemed to be blocking out the computer screen.

"You're losing it," she mumbled to herself. Duke had disrupted her sleep all night. Was he going to intrude on her concentration today, as well?

Nibbling on her thumbnail, she stared into space with a frown between her eyes. Why did she behave so differently with Duke than with other men? She had never been so waspish on a first date, and although she had denied it to Duke, she *was* the one who had ruined their evening. Why, for heaven's sake?

Confusing her even more was the way she had completely lost her senses in his arms. After hardly being nice to him all evening, she had kissed him back with a passion she hadn't even known she was capable of feeling. Oh, his kisses, she thought with a melting sensation. No wonder she had barely slept last night.

He had said he would be calling, but would he?

Even more disturbing to contemplate, was she hoping he would?

A surge of self-annoyance had her grimacing. Not knowing her own mind was distracting and irritating, a most peculiar deviation from the confident clear thinker she had always been.

No, that wasn't completely true. She had become independent and self-sufficient after her parents' death. Before that tragic event, she had been a normal, happy-go-lucky child with a very strong dependence on her mother and father.

Lola sighed softly and sadly at the thought of her parents. A journey into her past never failed to include the one major crisis of her life. She had been so young, only eight, and all she'd known to do was cry. Then Uncle Charlie had appeared. He'd wiped her eyes and held her, and told her everything was going to be all right, and that she was going to come and live with him and Serena and Ron.

Only it hadn't happened that easily. The state of Texas— her family had lived in Dallas—had intervened. She was an orphan, and an investigation of Charlie, blood relative or not, was deemed necessary to find out if he would be a fit guardian. It was a point not covered in her parents' wills, strange when they had been so diligent about her inheriting their material possessions when she reached the age of eighteen.

While social workers and family court judges were deciding her fate, she had been put into foster care. Letters and phone calls from Charlie, Serena and Ron were her lifeline. Her initial foster home became a second, then a third. Some of the people had been nice to her, some had not. At first she had been cowed by it all, but after a few months she began relying more and more on herself. Her youth had precluded an understanding of the legal process, but she felt that she understood one thing very well: she was all alone in a very large world.

When Charlie was finally awarded her guardianship, she was a somber little girl who looked to no one else for anything. He had helped her pack her clothes, and said funny things to try to make her smile.

The finale to that awful time was arriving in Rocky Ford, being greeted and welcomed by Ron and Serena, getting settled into the bedroom Charlie had given her for her very own, and ultimately, after a few months, beginning to feel like a part of the family. The truth was, though, that those fourteen months in foster care had drastically changed her; there was a portion of her makeup that would forever remain separate and independent. Charlie, Serena and Ron had accepted her the way she was, and they had all grown to love one another very much.

Lola started, as though coming awake. The cursor on the computer screen was blinking at her, reminding her that she had work to do.

Putting both the past and Duke Sheridan out of her mind, she got to it.

Duke had risen early, worked all morning with his men and come to the house for lunch around twelve-thirty. Then he went to his office to go through the mail. There was always a stack of mail on his desk, most of it merely needing a quick glance before being tossed into the wastebasket. But some letters and any bills required attention and he piled those on his left. To his right was the telephone, and his gaze kept drifting to the instrument.

Lola would be at her store and he wanted to call her. But he wouldn't put it past her to hang up on him, and he wasn't sure he wanted to give her the chance. Why in hell couldn't he get her out of his mind? She was pretty, yes, but so were a million other women. Dropping an unopened envelope, he tapped his fingers on the top of the desk, glaring at the phone as if his quandary were somehow its fault.

His uncertainty was aggravating, probably because he was rarely uncertain about anything. But Lola not only had his motor running, she had him going in circles.

Getting up, he marched around the room. It had rich, dark paneling, a rock fireplace, hunter green carpet, leather sofa and chairs, and oak file cabinets and desk. It was his favorite room in the house, the place where he normally did his best thinking—other than on the back of a horse—but today he was having trouble putting two thoughts together wherever he was.

His state of mind was Lola's fault, he thought irately. Last night could have—*should* have—been wonderful, and she hadn't allowed it. So why couldn't he just put it behind him, forget the whole thing and go on as though he had never met Lola Fanon?

That idea caused his body to uncomfortably tense up. He didn't *want* to forget the whole thing. He didn't *want* to go on as though he'd never met Lola. She wasn't just another woman, dammit, she was...she was...

Hell, he didn't know what she was, other than an itch he couldn't scratch. Shaking his head at his own ambivalence, he returned to the desk and sat down. This time he didn't give himself room to question and doubt what he was doing. Reaching for the phone, he dialed the number of the Men's Western Wear store.

After two rings the voice he wanted to hear was in his ear. "Men's Western Wear, Lola speaking."

Duke answered in a mellow, confident tone, a far cry from how he was feeling. "Hi, beautiful."

"Duke?" Lola's pulse suddenly went wild. He had called. Was it a curse or a blessing? With Duke, she just didn't know, but there was still a gladness in her system that hadn't been there a minute ago.

"Right on the first try," Duke drawled. "How are you today?"

"Uh, fine. And you?"

"Not so fine. Lola, I've thought about last night ever since I dropped you off. I don't know what caused it, but something sure put us on the wrong footing. I'd like to apologize for anything I might have done to offend you.''

"I . . . I owe you an apology, too." She hadn't thought of apologizing before this, but it seemed like the right thing to do. If he could be that big, so could she. "I'm really not the witch I seemed to be last night."

He laughed softly. "I never thought you were a witch, honey, not even once. Listen, how about coming out to the ranch for dinner tonight?"

"Your ranch?" She knew exactly which ranch he was talking about; she wasn't that dense. But his invitation was so surprising that she needed a few seconds to think about it.

"Of course my ranch," he said with another laugh. "Were you ever out here, maybe years ago when you were a kid?"

"No, I'm sure I wasn't." She really would like to see the Sheridan Ranch, see where Duke lived, *how* Duke lived.

But her curiosity waned when she thought of the two of them having dinner alone in his home.

"Do you cook?" she asked uneasily.

"Me?" Duke laughed. "Afraid not, honey. I can boil up a hot dog, if I have to, and make a pot of coffee, but I leave the cooking to June."

"June is your cook?"

"June Hansen. Her husband, Rufe, works as handyman on the place. They've lived on the ranch for a long time."

"They live there?" A married couple living in Duke's home put a whole other light on his dinner invitation in Lola's estimation. Surely he wouldn't try anything funny with other people in the house.

"For about fifteen years," Duke affirmed. "The Hansens are like family to me. Anyway, June's a great cook and I guarantee a good meal. How about it?" He happened to glance at one of the room's windows. "Hey, it's finally raining. Been threatening rain all morning, and it's really starting to come down. It would probably be best if I drove in and picked you up. Wouldn't want you having car trouble or something in the rain."

"It probably won't last that long, Duke."

"Possibly, but you never know. Tell you what. If it's still raining at six, I'll come and pick you up. If not, you can drive out on your own. Do you know the way?"

"I'm sure Charlie can tell me."

"Well, just in case he can't, I'll give you directions."

Lola wrote furiously as Duke told her how to go.

"And when you see a sign that says Sheridan Ranch, take the next right turn. That's my driveway. It's about another mile to the house."

"Okay, I think I have it." It had to be about thirty miles to the ranch.

"But if it's still raining, don't start out. I'll pick you up at Charlie's."

"Duke, I'm perfectly capable of driving in rain."

"But I'd feel a lot better about it if you didn't."

Did she care how he felt about it? Wasn't he behaving a little too possessively again?

Then again, she might be being overly sensitive when he truly could be thinking only of her safety. She frowned. Why did she constantly analyze everything he said and everything she thought where he was concerned? Was it a matter of trust? Did she trust him or didn't she? If not, she should be refusing this invitation instead of writing down directions to get to his ranch.

Vexed with herself again, she agreed. "All right, fine. If it's still raining at six, I'll wait for your arrival."

"Thanks, sweetheart. I'm sure glad I worked up the courage to call. Everything's going to be fine between us now, don't you think?"

"I...I don't know how to answer that," she stammered, a little taken aback by his inference.

He chuckled in her ear, a soft, caressing sound that raised goose bumps on her skin.

"You can answer it tonight. How's that?"

She smiled weakly. "You're sure about the Hansens living at the ranch. I mean, you wouldn't be pulling my leg about that, would you?"

"It's the God's truth, honey. June and Rufe Hansen live on the ranch. I swear it."

"Okay, I believe you. Duke, I'm sorry but I have to run. The store is full of people. See you tonight."

"Tonight," he repeated softly. Hanging up, he sat back with a smile of satisfaction. It had gone so well he could hardly believe it, but he sure as hell wasn't going to question Lola's change of heart.

Getting to his feet, he went to find June. He wanted a very special dinner this evening, and he knew June would be thrilled to help him out.

It rained all afternoon. Business started slowing down around three as people put shopping aside to go home and get out of the storm. At four Lola sent one of her employees home—on Saturdays she always had two clerks—asked the other one to call her if by some chance she was needed, and then returned to her office to finish her inventory work.

When a shipment of jeans, shirts or what have you came in, each item was tagged with an identification number that was then entered into the computer as an In item. That same number was written on sales invoices, which was then put into the computer program as an Out item. It was a simple but very effective system of inventory control. Anytime she was up-to-date on entering the sales invoices, she could print out a list of every piece of merchandise that should still be on the racks and shelves.

That list was important information. From it, she knew when it was necessary to order more shirts or boots, for instance. Also, she could make a physical count of the merchandise in the store, compare it with the computer list and find out if anything was missing. Shoplifting was a problem to reckon with in any retail sales establishment, and it happened occasionally, even though she and her employees did their best to stay alert.

She was through with the sales invoices at five, printed out the list and then shut down the computer. Setting the list aside for later perusal, she went into the main part of the store. Karen Lafferty was tidying racks.

"Any business at all?" Lola asked.

"Only one man came in. He bought a pair of jeans," Karen replied.

Lola walked to the bank of front windows and looked out. "It's still pouring." It was also getting dark. Passing cars—the few that there were—had their headlights on. There wasn't a pedestrian in sight. When looking for space in which to put her store, she had felt fortunate to find this location, as it was in the busiest part of town.

It wasn't busy now. She had known there would be bad weather days with very few customers, but this was her first. And it felt eerie...the rain streaming down the windows, the dim circles of slowly moving headlights, the emptiness of the street and sidewalks. No one was even going into or leaving Herb's Diner next door, which was always busy. A shiver went up her spine, but she ignored it and told herself, firmly, that there was nothing eerie about a hard rainfall in Montana.

She turned to look at her youthful clerk. "Karen, you can leave, if you want. There's really no reason for you to hang around when there's nothing to do."

Karen nodded. "All right. But I'd be glad to stay until closing. I mean, maybe you'd rather not be alone in the store for another hour."

"No problem. You run along." While Karen was getting her things, Lola removed all the cash from the register except for approximately one hundred dollars, put it in an envelope and brought it to the safe in her office.

Showing Karen out the back door, which she then made sure was securely locked, although it always was, Lola returned to the front of the store.

She straightened racks and shelves that were already neat, just for something to do. And she kept glancing at her watch. Whether or not that eerie feeling she had was silly, she couldn't shake it. It was growing darker outside, and the rain showed no sign of letting up.

Deliberately she turned her thoughts to Duke and the evening ahead. But that made her think of calling him and canceling dinner at his ranch. They could do it on another night, when neither of them would have to drive in a downpour.

She didn't make the call. Instead, she leaned on the counter, doodled on a pad and *thought* about making it. What would he say? What would she say? *Duke, it's raining so hard, let's have dinner at the ranch another time.*

Sighing, she straightened and laid down the pen. Maybe she was merely looking for an excuse to cancel. She felt so torn over Duke, wanting to see him, not wanting to see him. Was she afraid of him, as he'd dared to suggest last night? Afraid of where he might lead her with his potent kisses and bold caresses?

She nearly jumped out of her skin when the bell above the door jangled and a man walked in. He was wearing a long black slicker and a big hat riding low on his forehead.

"Hello," she said, forcing cheerfulness into her greeting. "Wet out there, isn't it?"

"Yeah," he said without a trace of a smile.

Lola walked around the counter. "Could I help you find something?" He was looking around the store, as though with a specific item in mind. That eerie feeling she'd been battling was making her skin crawl, but even though this man made her terribly uncomfortable, she couldn't be rude to a customer. Just because he looked like a desperado didn't mean that he wasn't an ordinary citizen.

I'm afraid! A second thought was stunning: she hadn't been afraid of anything or anyone since moving in with Uncle Charlie as a child. Certainly she wasn't afraid of Duke; the mere idea was absurd. In fact, if he came walking through that door right now, she would love him forever.

But he wasn't going to walk in; he was going to pick her up at home. Besides, there were all kinds of fear, and what she was feeling now because of a dark, unfriendly stranger couldn't be compared to emotional upheavals that made one wary and uneasy.

"We have a very nice selection of jeans," she said, wincing internally because she had spoken too loudly. Whatever she was feeling, she had to appear strong and unafraid. Predators preyed on the weak, she told herself.

"I'll just look around," the man grunted.

"Certainly." Lola faked a smile. "Browse all you like." Taking a position near the counter, she watched the man walk among the stock. It was so quiet, she could hear his every movement. Most of the time the radio was playing, wafting country music throughout the store. Karen must have turned it off.

From the boot section he called, "You here all alone?"

Lola's heart skipped a beat. "Not at all. My husband is working in the back."

"Your husband? How come you ain't wearing a ring?"

"Umm, I don't wear it during working hours." Her head was swimming, lies mingling with intensifying fear. "It's . . . an expensive ring and I . . . I don't want it damaged, so I leave it at home."

The man began walking toward her. He stopped about four feet away. "Call him."

She blinked. "Call him?"

"Your husband. Have him come up here."

A nervous laugh gurgled out of her mouth. "Whatever for? He's busy." She saw in his narrowed eyes that he didn't believe her, and in the next moment became aware of something in his hand. There was a click, and a long, shiny blade sprang from the handle of the knife he was holding. Her heart nearly stopped. "What do you want?"

"What do you think I want? Open that cash register and be quick about it."

A peculiar calmness descended upon her. With her head held high, she walked around the counter and pressed the combination of buttons that opened the cash drawer.

"Now . . . move out of the way," the man growled. "And don't try anything funny."

Lola stepped back, then scooted around to the front side of the counter. The man dipped his left hand into the cash drawer and scooped up the bills. He mumbled a vile curse. "Where's the rest? You got a safe somewhere in here?"

"There's a safe, yes, but I only work here and I don't know the combination." If he was really a stranger to the area, he wouldn't know she owned the store.

"Let me see it."

"It's in the back."

"You go first. I'll be right behind you."

Fear wasn't freezing her now. She was thinking clearly and knew she couldn't go in the back with him. He was still on the other side of the counter. Whirling, she ran for the door. He yelled a vicious curse and ran after her, but she hit the door hard. It swung open and she dashed out into the rain and ran next door to the diner.

"Herb..." she gasped, barely able to breathe. Herb was a burly man of fifty-odd years. There were three people sitting at his counter. "A man...in my store...he has a knife..."

Herb reached under the counter and came out with an enormous pistol. "Call the cops," he told her, and headed out into the rain.

The people left their stools and huddled around her. "Sit down," one said. "You're pale as a ghost, young woman. I'll call the police. Joe, get her a drink of water."

She realized then how wet she'd gotten during her mad dash to Herb's Diner. Her clothes were sticking to her; she was shivering uncontrollably, both from the aftermath of trauma and getting drenched.

Herb walked in. "Whoever he was, he hightailed it, Lola. No one's in the store now. Did anyone call the police?"

"I did," someone said. "Dispatch said they'd send a car right away."

From somewhere Herb produced a blanket, which he placed around Lola's shaking shoulders. Next a cup of hot coffee was put in her hand. "What'd that guy look like?" Herb asked.

"Tall. And dark. He was wearing a long black slicker."

"I'm gonna call Charlie," Herb said. "He should know."

"No...no, please, Herb. He'll just get all upset, and it's over. As soon as the police get here I'm going to lock up and go home. Please, I'll be fine." Warmth was returning to her body. And normalcy. It had been a bad experience, but she had used her head and survived it.

Two uniformed police officers walked in. "What's going on, Herb?" one of them asked.

"This lady is Lola Fanon, Gary. Owns the men's store next door. A man..."

"Let's let her tell it, Herb." The officer turned to Lola. "What happened, Ms. Fanon?"

An hour later, the two cops escorted her to her car and followed her home. It didn't surprise her to see both Duke and Charlie come running out of the house. After all, it wasn't every day that a police car followed her home.

Six

As Lola didn't want to upset anyone, especially Charlie, she told her story to Charlie and Duke calmly and without dramatics. The two men listened raptly, though with much different reactions. Charlie was a hundred percent concerned about her, and his dear face conveyed only that to Lola. Was she all right? Thank God she hadn't been hurt, or worse. It was as though he couldn't reassure him enough that she had come through the frightening event unscathed.

Duke's expression, on the other hand, grew darker with every word she spoke, until Lola realized that he was seething with suppressed anger.

"Then someone in Herb's called the police," she said, feeling that she had reached the end of the story. "And here I am, safe and sound," she added with a smile at her uncle. "I'm really all right, Charlie."

"And thank the good Lord you are," he responded ardently.

Duke's response was to get up from his chair and pace.

Lola's eyes followed him while Charlie praised her courage and quick-wittedness.

Finally, Duke stopped with his hands on his hips and a glower on his face. "You shouldn't have been in the store alone. Dammit, you should *never* be there alone!"

Lola's jaw dropped. He was angry with her, and she'd been thinking his fury was directed at the robber!

"I beg your pardon," she said icily. "I own that store and I have every right to be there alone."

"That attitude could have gotten you killed today," Duke snapped harshly. "You managed to get away this time, but what about the next?"

"The next?" she echoed incredulously. "Are you insinuating that I should live my life waiting for another moron to come into the store with a knife? I won't do it, Duke. I didn't like what happened today, and yes, it was a frightening experience, but I am not going to cower in corners and surround myself with clerks I can't afford and who wouldn't guarantee my safety, anyway. The same thing could happen to Charlie here. Many times he's alone in his business. Should he live in fear, as you're suggesting I do?"

"It's not the same thing. You're a woman."

Lola rolled her eyes. "Here we go again. You have a very warped opinion of women in today's world. I happen to be in business, and I intend to operate my business, as thousands, maybe millions, of other women do."

Charlie got up and cleared his throat. Clearly he was uncomfortable with Lola and Duke's argument. "Uh, you two excuse me, okay? I've got a few things to do." He left the room.

Lola glared at Duke. "Now see what you've done?"

He did see, quite suddenly and uneasily. But it seemed to him that Lola wasn't taking the robbery as seriously as she should. She wasn't weepy or shaken. Maybe she had been; there could have been omissions in her story. Right now, though—in fact, since she'd arrived home with a police escort—she was calm and collected. Her composure wasn't at all what he would have expected in any woman after such a traumatic experience.

Frowning, he went to kneel by her chair. "Lola, don't you understand what could have happened to you?"

The plea in his eyes softened her own expression. "Yes, I understand," she said quietly. "Do *you* understand that it didn't happen? Give me credit for how I handled the situation. I could have panicked. I could have caused the man to panic and do something he had no intention of doing. He wanted money. I opened the register for him. If the safe had been in the front of the store, I probably would have opened that for him, as well. I know my life is more important than money, and when he ordered me to go into the back with him I also knew that was where the real danger lay. I made a splitsecond decision. He was on the other side of the counter. I ran. I did the right thing. You should try to keep tonight in perspective. I kept cool, and I got away. Charlie's proud of what I did. The police applauded my reactions. You're the only one blaming me because I dared to be alone in my own place of business. That's unfair, Duke, very unfair."

He took her hand. "But the next time..."

"I am not going to worry about the next time," she said sharply, attempting to pull her hand away and failing. She sighed heavily. "I'd just as soon not talk about it anymore. I've said it all, several times, and right now I'd like to take a hot shower."

"I called June and told her we'd be a little late for dinner."

Lola started. "Oh, I forgot about that. Duke, it's still pouring outside. I really would like to cancel dinner tonight and—"

His eyes narrowed on her. "You *are* shaken up. You've been putting on an act, haven't you?"

"I most certainly have not. I'm fine and it's not an act."

"Then why cancel our plans? And don't blame it on the rain. You grew up in Rocky Ford, and you know as well as I do that the weather never stops anyone from doing anything around here. Anything they *want* to do, that is. You said you'd have dinner at the ranch, and June went to a lot of trouble to prepare a special meal. I would think..."

"All right! Give me a few minutes to get ready." This time when Lola tried to free her hand from his grasp, he let go. "Thank you," she said caustically.

Ignoring her tone, Duke stood up. "I'll talk to Charlie while you're getting ready." He knew he'd gone too far with Lola in Charlie's presence, possibly alarming the older man, which he'd never meant to do. Any alarm because of tonight should be Lola's, not Charlie's. Duke still didn't believe she grasped the danger she'd been in; a man didn't threaten someone with a knife unless he was prepared to use it. The subject was far from closed in Duke's mind, but he wouldn't argue with Lola about it in front of her uncle again.

Lola left the room. Charlie was somewhere in the house and Duke would find him. Let them talk about it man to man, she thought, entering her bedroom to undress and put on a robe before heading for the bathroom.

It was her reflection in the bathroom mirror that caused a small explosion in her system. Her hair was damp and stringy, and her face was a pasty white, even her lips. She began trembling, and she suddenly had to sit on the commode as her legs felt too weak to hold her weight.

I could have been killed. It was finally catching up with her, that eerie feeling she'd had before sending Karen home, the dark stranger walking in, the fear she'd felt, and then the peculiar calmness. She thought about the man, and seeing him in her mind's eye, feeling his presence again, caused her trembling to increase.

She had given the police his description, and there was some comfort in telling herself that they would find the man and arrest him. His hat had been so low she never had gotten a really good look at his eyes, but . . .

Her mouth dropped open. That scar on the left side of his chin! She remembered it very distinctly, but had forgotten it until now. Rising on shaky legs, she hurried back to her room and the bedside phone. Awkwardly because her hands were so unsteady, she looked up the number of the police department in the phone book and dialed it. A man answered. "Rocky Ford Police Department."

Lola drew a breath. "This is Lola Fanon. My store was robbed tonight and two officers came to investigate. I can't remember their names, but it's urgent that I talk to one of them."

"Hold on a minute."

In a few seconds, Lola heard, "Miss Fanon? This is Officer Gary Anderson. What can I do for you?"

"I just remembered something else about the man who robbed me. He has a scar on the left side of his chin."

"Is that so?" Officer Anderson said with satisfaction in his voice. "Now I'm sure we have the right man. I was going to call you, Miss Fanon. We picked up a guy at the truck stop west of town. He fit your description and had no vehicle of his own. He was trying to catch a ride with a trucker. Anyway, we'd like you to come to the station in the morning and make a positive ID."

"Are you saying you already found and arrested him?"

"We booked him on vagrancy, just to hold him until we could check him out, Miss Fanon. But that information about the scar on his chin cinches it. He's our man, I'm sure of it."

"Well . . . that certainly was fast work." An enormous relief surged through Lola's body. "Thank you. Yes, I'll come by the station in the morning. Any particular time?"

"Around ten should do it. Unless . . . well, tomorrow's Sunday. If that's your usual time to attend church . . ."

"I'll skip church tomorrow and see you at ten. And thank you again."

Lola put down the phone and realized that she was no longer trembling. In fact, she felt like celebrating. Not in her wildest dreams could she have imagined the police would move so quickly. The guy was in jail. In jail!

"Oh, thank God," she whispered, knowing now that she had harbored a deeply buried fear that he might come after her again. Part of her composure with Charlie and Duke *had* been an act. Not all of it, but she hadn't wanted Charlie worrying about her every time she left the house, which she knew he was perfectly capable of doing.

Duke, now, was another story. He had seen through her bravado, which was disturbing as he shouldn't know her well enough to be that perceptive, considering the few times they'd been together.

Reflecting on it all, Lola returned to the bathroom for her shower. Meanwhile, in the living room, Duke and Charlie were talking.

"I'm sorry I started an argument with Lola in your home, Charlie. I'm sure she won't thank me for it."

"Probably not," Charlie agreed, giving Duke a somber look. "Do you really think she shouldn't be in that store alone?"

Duke cleared his throat. He'd worried this man enough for one night. "She proved she can take care of herself, Charlie. I was way out of line."

"Well, she always could, you know. Take care of herself, I mean. Insisted on it, in fact. Those fourteen months in foster care were hard on her. She was such a little thing, and—"

Duke's ears pricked up. "Foster care? When was that, Charlie?"

"Right after her folks died." Charlie let a second go by. "My brother and his wife. Jim and I were always close. It was a hard loss to bear, but there was Lola to think about. I went to Texas, where they lived—Dallas—thinking I could just bring her home with me. The state had other ideas, and they took their sweet time about it, too. Fourteen months of shunting Lola from pillar to post. Hell of a system, if you ask me."

"Why'd they take so long?"

Charlie shifted his weight in his chair. "Aw, they laid it on an investigation of me, to find out if I'd be a fit guardian for my own little niece. Damnation, I love her like my own, Duke. Always did. Bureaucracy and red tape. Damned nonsense. Anyway, there were people snooping around town, asking questions about me. And they even knocked on my door and requested financial information. You see, Lola was left a sizable sum from her parents' estate, and I guess they thought I might want to get my hands on it.

Guess there are some people who do things like that," Charlie said disgustedly.

"I'm sure there are," Duke quietly agreed. There was a noticeable ache in his heart for a little, dark-haired, green-eyed girl who had probably thought for fourteen long months that no one wanted her. He nearly choked up at that picture. Her mother and father were dead, and her only relatives, Charlie and his kids, lived two thousand miles away.

"Did she know you were doing everything you could to get her?" he asked.

"I told her so in letters and on the phone, but she was just a little kid, Duke." Charlie shook his head. "It was hard on her, make no mistake."

Duke nodded. "I'm sure it was. But she adjusted to living with you and your family, didn't she?"

"Adjusted real well. But she always held something back, Duke, something that was private and hers alone. Never did know what to call it, but it made her a little different. I think maybe it was why she wandered the way she did after college." Charlie smiled then. "She came back home, though, and she seems real happy to be here. She's a special woman, Duke," he added with a direct look into Duke's eyes.

"I think so, too, Charlie," Duke said quietly.

The two men regarded each other silently for several moments, then Charlie said, "Yes, I believe you do."

Lola walked in. "You believe what, Uncle Charlie?"

Both men got to their feet. Charlie chuckled. "Now you really don't expect me to tell you *all* my secrets, do you?" he said teasingly.

"I didn't know you had any secrets." Lola, too, spoke in a teasing vein.

She looked so beautiful in her cherry red raincoat that Duke couldn't help staring. She glanced his way. "Exchanging secrets, hmm?"

Duke grinned. "Guess you caught us."

Lola slung the strap of her bag over her shoulder. "Well, I'm ready to go. Incidentally, I talked to the police again— I called them because I remembered a detail I'd omitted in the robber's description—and Officer Anderson informed me that they already have the man in custody. I'm to go to the station in the morning to make a positive ID.''

"Well, that's the best news I've heard all day," Charlie exclaimed. "They got him already. Imagine that."

"Incredible," Duke murmured. "Appears that our police department is on the ball." His remarks were purely automatic. He didn't like any of this, not Lola being robbed, not her having to ID a criminal who might or might not be convicted. He wanted her safe and sound, protected from life's harsher realities, such as some son of a bitch walking into her store and threatening her with a knife. He'd give anything he had if she would get rid of that damned store— sell it, lease it out or give it away, it was all the same to him. Just so she would never again be exposed to another such incident as today's.

He offered his hand to Charlie. "Lola's ready, so we'd better get going. Good talking to you, Charlie."

Charlie nodded. "Drive safely."

"Will do."

"Night, Charlie." Lola kissed her uncle's cheek.

They made it to Duke's four-wheeler without getting too wet and settled themselves in the front seat. Duke started the motor and the windshield wipers.

"Still coming down in buckets," he said. "Could be some flooding from rain this hard." He backed out of the driveway and onto the street.

Lola rode without speaking, recalling that one of the reasons she'd given herself for accepting Duke's dinner invitation was to see his ranch. She wasn't going to see much of it on a pitch-black, rain-soaked night like this, she thought wryly.

But it really was only one of her reasons for accepting, she knew; Duke himself was the other. She was drawn to him regardless of his faults and flaws, and he had them, that was certain. Take his nervy outspokenness tonight, for instance.

"I really didn't appreciate your remarks and opinions about the robbery in front of Charlie," she said coolly.

"I should have waited until we were alone," Duke concurred. "But I only said what I felt then and still do." He sent her a quick glance. "Why don't you get rid of that store?"

"That's a ridiculous idea," she said scornfully. "I worked very hard to turn an empty, bare-walled building into an attractive, successful business, and one bad experience is not going to ruin it for me." She was watching out the windshield through the quick, smooth sweeps of the wipers, looking at the wet, black road and what she could see of the soggy countryside. There was very little traffic. In spite of Duke's comment about Montanans doing what they wanted regardless of the weather, most people had sense enough to stay home on a night like this. "I can't believe that your solution to problems that might arise in the path of your own success is to give up," she said.

"You're right. But that's me and my problems. I'm talking about you and your problems."

"My problems are none of your business, Duke," she said a bit sharply. "Putting it even more bluntly, my *business* is none of your business. Stay out of it. Especially in front of Charlie."

"An ultimatum," Duke said with a grim expression. "Why is it that you and I can't have a conversation without anger? We didn't start out arguing."

"If you're angry, it's only because you don't like being told what to do. I think I have a right to safeguard my uncle from reckless, unnecessary remarks that will only worry him."

"I already admitted I should have waited to talk about it until we were alone. What else do you want me to say?"

"I *don't* want you telling me in a macho, overly protective manner that I should get rid of the store."

Duke's jaw clenched. "Damn, you're a hard woman to talk to. I was not trying to be macho and overly protective, but if that's what it sounded like to you, what's so terrible about it? Men *should* protect women."

Lola gave a brief, impolite laugh. "I'm sure there are women who appreciate and even relish that attitude. I just don't happen to be one of them."

"No, you prefer wimps who ask how high when you tell them to jump."

"And you dared to wonder why we can't have a conversation without anger? How about because you're overbearing, smug, opinionated and stubborn as a mule?"

"How about because I care about you, and you've got a snotty, smart-ass answer to everything I say?" he shot back.

"Then why do you care about me?" she snapped at him.

He drew in a long, exasperated breath. "I've been trying to figure that one out myself."

They both fell silent. Duke was driving cautiously. There was standing water in low spots of the road, huge puddles to get through without stalling the engine, but he wasn't thinking of that. His thoughts were on the woman next to him, and he gritted his teeth as he realized that he couldn't *stop* caring for her, however much he wished it.

Lola's thoughts were startlingly similar. What was happening with her and Duke? She didn't have to be in this car with him tonight. No one had forced her to accept his dinner invitation, and yet, here she was. His after-shave and her perfume mingled into one unnerving scent. Despite the anger that kept popping up between them and the rainy, dark night outside, the interior of the vehicle had a warm, sensual quality. Was chemistry stronger than conflicting attitudes?

Swallowing hard, Lola tried to put that chemistry idea out of her mind. But once born it wasn't easily eradicated. Like it or not, she knew now that it was chemistry that had brought about that disturbingly passionate interlude the other night. Obviously they could shriek at each other one minute and go wild with desire in the next. What a dismal picture that thought presented. She didn't want a relationship with a guy who thought women were hothouse flowers who couldn't possibly make a sensible decision without a man's wise and wonderful input.

So, she concluded uneasily, *I'm not entirely in control with Duke, am I?* Other forces were at work here, things with which she had no experience. Those forces could consist of nature, chemistry or just plain lust, she thought, and then tensed because she didn't like any one of those terms.

Heaving a sigh, she turned her head to stare out the side window, though all she could see was rain running down the glass and a shadowy reflection of her own face.

Duke made a turn. "This is my driveway. We're almost there." He glanced in Lola's direction and saw the back of her head. "Are you all right?"

She faced front. "Yes, I'm all right. Why wouldn't I be?"

"Lola," he said with a discouraged sigh. "I don't want to argue anymore."

After a moment, she said wearily, "Neither do I. But I will tell you this. I wish I had stayed home tonight. You and I are very different people, Duke, and you make me uncomfortable."

"I might make you uncomfortable, but it's not because we're different from each other. Quite the opposite, in fact. You're more like me than anyone else I've ever known. You think like a man."

"I what?"

"You heard me. At the same time you're thinking like a man, you're so physically female you're driving me nuts. What kind of perfume are you wearing?"

Feeling suddenly drained and deflated, Lola let her head drop back against the seat. There was no way to win with Duke, though what she hoped to win escaped her. It was just that he always seemed to be two steps ahead of her, and she wasn't used to being around anyone, man or woman, who was that quick on the comeback.

"I'm nothing at all like you," she said evenly, vowing to keep her temper in check. "And I don't appreciate the comparison. Another thing, I do not believe that men's and women's brains work on different planes, so if you were intending to either flatter or insult me by telling me I think like a man, you didn't succeed."

Duke pulled the four-wheeler to a stop and turned off the ignition. "We're here. Before we go in, let me say that I wasn't trying to flatter *or* insult you. I was merely stating a fact as I see it. I'm sorry you wish you had stayed home. I hope June's good cooking changes your mind. Come on. Let's make a run for it so we don't get drenched."

Raising her head, Lola saw the blurred but bright lights of many windows. They were parked close to the house, and from what she could see through the rain, every room seemed to be beaming light into the dark, dreary night.

"Will we be heading north or south when we get out?" she asked dryly, referring to the front or back of the house.

Duke laughed with genuine amusement. "I like your off-beat sense of humor. We'll be heading north. It'll take us to the back door of the house."

"Let's go, then." Lola opened her door.

They dashed to the back of the house and ran up three stairs that put them on a long redwood porch with a roof. It was well lighted, and dry except for the very edges of the decking.

"This is nice," Lola said, noticing the patio furniture while shaking raindrops from the fabric of her raincoat. She could also see into several lighted rooms of the house, those that shared the exterior wall with the wide wood porch. The kitchen looked homey and inviting, and the other room on view was a dining room with a long table bearing a creamy linen tablecloth, a floral centerpiece and two place settings.

Frowning, she turned to ask Duke why there were only two settings. Weren't the Hansens going to eat with them? But Duke was already opening the door for her. "You first," he said with a smile.

Nodding, she stepped past him and into an entry hall that contained wall hooks and hangers.

"Let me have your coat," Duke said while removing and hanging his jacket and hat on two of the hooks.

"Thank you." Lola started to slip the coat from her shoulders, but Duke was suddenly standing at her back to do it for her. Her breath caught at his nearness. She could have told him that he was touching her much more than was necessary to help a person out of a coat, but she made no comment.

"This way," Duke said then, moving around her to lead her into the kitchen, which smelled wonderful.

"Where's June?" Lola asked, looking around at the obviously vacant room.

Duke shrugged. "Probably at home. Let's see what's in the oven. Smells great, doesn't it?"

Lola stiffened. "Excuse me, but didn't you say that June and her husband live on the ranch?"

Duke glanced over his shoulder at her. "They do." He pulled out a roaster containing two plump, browned chickens. "Ah, this looks good." Using pot holders, he carried the roaster to the counter.

"Wait a minute," Lola said. "They live on the ranch, but they went home? Would you mind explaining that?"

Duke slowly turned around to face her. "You thought they lived in this house?"

"I was under that impression, yes. How do you suppose I got that impression?"

Duke looked away. "Aw, hell. Lola, I didn't intentionally mislead you. You asked if they lived on the ranch and it never entered my mind that you were talking about them living with me. They have their own house." He drew a breath that sounded genuinely uneasy to Lola. "Is this going to ruin dinner for you?"

"I'm wondering if I should believe you. We're alone in this house, aren't we?"

He hesitated, but finally answered. "Yes."

Alone on a dark and stormy night. Had he connived and lied to get her out here, deliberately omitting the rather important fact of the Hansens having their own house when he'd assured her they lived on the ranch?

Duke's expression was beseeching. She looked so pretty in a red-and-black print dress. He liked that she wore dresses, and he liked her. So much. And yet he couldn't seem to do anything right with her. He had not intentionally misled her, maybe because he was so used to his and the

Hansens' routines that it hadn't occurred to him to explain them.

But could he convince Lola of that?

His lips tightened. Convincing Lola of anything was damned near impossible. She would have to draw her own conclusion about this and live with it.

"Why don't you take a look at the rest of the house while I put the food on the table?" he said quietly. "I'll have everything ready in a few minutes, then we can eat."

"Fine," she said tonelessly, and turned on her heel and walked out. It might be impolite not to offer to help with the food, but she really didn't give a damn. Not when Duke had just given her a very sound reason to doubt him.

Seven

As ambiguous as Lola felt toward Duke, she couldn't resist a quick tour of his house. It had been constructed on three levels, two steps down into a sunken living room with a high beamed ceiling and a striking white rock fireplace, five steps up into the bedroom wing, and then the level that contained the kitchen, dining room, laundry, a guest bathroom and a den. The den was also an office, she decided from the desk and file cabinets. All in all it was a lovely, spacious house, nicely furnished and decorated, and immaculate.

She was on her way back to the kitchen when Duke called, "Lola? Everything's ready for dinner."

"I'm coming."

They went into the dining room, and Duke pulled out the chair at the place setting to the right of the one at the head of the table. With a murmured "Thank you," Lola sat down, picked up her linen napkin, shook out the folds and laid it in her lap. Duke took his seat.

"Well, this is nice," he said with a congenial smile.

Refuting his comment would be argumentative and untrue. The platters and bowls of food looked and smelled wonderful. There was soft background music mingling with the sound of rain on the roof. Her dinner companion was handsome beyond words and obviously trying very hard to make her feel at ease.

Lola sighed inwardly. However suspicious she felt about Duke's method of getting her out here, was there any point to dwelling on it? They would only argue again and June's good dinner would be ruined.

"Yes, it's nice," she agreed. They began filling their plates. "I like your house." Lola felt it was a safe comment that also happened to be the truth.

Duke nodded. "Thanks, so do I. June does a great job of keeping it up." Instantly he wished he hadn't mentioned June, because there was a sudden chill in the air and a frosty glaze in Lola's eyes.

Reaching for the bottle of wine on the table, he filled their stemmed glasses. He raised his and, automatically, so did Lola lift hers.

"Cheers," he said, deliberately keeping the toast impersonal. It wasn't easy, not when personal was all he could think of with Lola. But apparently he couldn't completely be himself with her. Every time he tried to add warmth to their conversation she rebelled, for God knew what reason. Not that he planned to quit trying, but he was going to make dinner a pleasant event if he had to bite off his tongue to keep from saying something that would cause any more frosty expressions on Lola's beautiful face.

"Cheers," she responded coolly before taking a sip from her glass. The wine was delicious, and she took another sip before setting down her glass.

Besides being a safe topic, seeing his house had whetted her curiosity about the rest of the ranch. "You've lived here all your life?" she inquired, picking up her fork.

"Born and raised," Duke said. "I really can't imagine living anywhere else."

"And you raise cattle."

"Yes, ma'am. Some horses, too, but cattle are the main-stay of the ranch."

They were eating, talking between bites. The food was as good as it looked, and Lola found herself relaxing. The wine helped relieve her tension, as well. To be honest, it felt good to relax. The latter events of the day had wound her up as tightly as an eight-day clock, and each swallow of wine loosened the spring a little more.

It pleased Duke to see her smile every so often, and once she even laughed, when he told her about the time a bull escaped its pen and chased two ranch hands up a tree.

"That was a long time ago," Duke said with a reminiscent glow in his eyes. "I remember Dad laughing fit to kill, then getting a pole from the barn and walking right up to that bull. He slid the pole through the ring in the bull's nose and brought that huge animal to its knees."

"You really do put rings in bulls' noses to control them?"

"We did then. Nowadays, we rely more on artificial insemination than on bulls. There are a few on the place, but they're pastured about a mile from the buildings. And they're not mean. I doubt if they'd chase anyone up a tree, at any rate." He chuckled. "But that old bull had the disposition of a hornet. And he liked only one thing."

"Which was?"

Duke chuckled again. "Cows."

Lola laughed again. "I see."

He liked her laugh, which he didn't hear often enough. Looking at her, he drew in a silent breath and realized that he liked everything about her. Even her spirited personality and go-to-hell attitude. No one would ever put a ring in her nose, would they?

But then, no one would put a ring in his nose, either. As he'd told her, they were very much alike, each of them strong-willed and self-reliant. The thought was simultaneously gratifying and disturbing; their relationship might be a little less rocky if they *weren't* so much alike.

"Dessert?" he asked when they had eaten their fill of the main dishes.

Lola shook her head. "Not for me, thanks. You go ahead, though."

"I'm stuffed. Let's have coffee in the living room."

"I'd like to clear the table and do the dishes first," Lola said.

"We don't have to do that."

"Duke, I'm not going to leave the kitchen and dining room in a mess for your housekeeper. And this leftover food should be put away." Pushing back her chair, Lola got to her feet.

Her look of determination deterred Duke's urge to explain that June expected to clean up in the morning. When he'd called to tell her they would be arriving at the ranch later than planned, she had told him to enjoy the evening with his guest and not to worry about the dishes.

But he wasn't going to start an argument over anything, particularly over something as mundane as doing the dishes. To hasten the project, he jumped in and helped. In fifteen minutes the food was in covered containers in the refrigerator and the kitchen was neat and clean.

"Now for that coffee," he said, drying his hands on a paper towel.

Lola was looking out the window. "It's still pouring. Maybe we should skip coffee. You have to drive me all the way to town and then come back, and it's getting wetter outside by the minute. You could run into a problem with the roads."

Every word she'd spoken was true, or at least possible. But the rain really wasn't what was bothering her; prolonging the evening was. He was going to make a pass, she was sure of it, and given her reaction the first time he'd kissed her, there was no telling what might happen in this big empty house.

"After that wine I need a cup of coffee before driving," Duke said, which Lola didn't believe for a second. He'd drunk maybe a glass and a half of wine, and they hadn't used large glasses, either. She'd consumed much more of the bottle than he had, and *she* certainly wasn't tipsy. Neither was he, the big phony.

But he definitely had the upper hand. She was, after all, miles from town in a record-breaking rainfall.

"All right, one cup," she conceded. "Excuse me for a few minutes while I freshen up." Taking her purse from the counter where she had laid it earlier, she headed for the guest bathroom.

"I'll be waiting for you in the living room," Duke called after her.

"I'm sure you will," she muttered under her breath, closing the bathroom door. After touching up her makeup, she caught the frown on her face in the mirror. It was there because of Duke, she thought, because she was in his home and he was waiting in the living room for her. For the same reasons, there seemed to be a knot of nervousness in her stomach. He had accused her of being afraid of him, and she was beginning to think he was right.

But wasn't that a little ludicrous? He was hardly brandishing a knife at her, after all.

Thinking of the robbery weakened her again, and she sat on the small ornate chair in the corner of the bathroom. This afternoon might haunt her off and on for the rest of her life, but it had been real, the knife had been real. The fear had been real . . . and sensible. Fearing Duke was not.

It wasn't the same feeling at all, she chided herself, not even close. And yet she had contrived some sort of emotional hurdle between Duke and herself, whether one called it fear or good sense.

But the whole thing had adolescent overtones, and she was years away from girlish skittishness. Besides, boys and men had never frightened her at any age. The truth was that if she really didn't like Duke, she wouldn't be here. Men did not talk her into dinner dates in their own home, especially those whom she found unappealing.

And Duke liked her. Along with his flirtatious and flattering remarks, she sensed his liking. If she admitted that she liked him, too, would she be putting herself in the "fair game" category? Just how far did Duke want this relationship to go? More important, how far did *she* want it to go? Dammit, why didn't she know her own mind with Duke?

Sighing, she got up and took a final look in the mirror. What to do, she thought uneasily, what to do. Picking up her purse, she left the bathroom and wended her way through the house to the living room.

There was a fire crackling in the fireplace. The ceiling light had been turned off and the room was softly lit by several lamps. A silver tray with a coffeepot, a small pitcher of cream and two cups resided on a table. Next to it was a crystal decanter containing an amber liquid.

The setting was lovely... and very romantic. Lola's heart fluttered in her chest. Mostly she was a pragmatic person, but what woman could completely deny romance? And it wasn't that she wanted to, either. She just had this strange edginess when it came to Duke, feeling as if she were being pulled in two different directions, and thus far she hadn't been able to figure out why.

Duke was kneeling in front of the fire, laying a log on the grate. Sensing her presence, he turned to watch her step down the two stairs to the living room level.

"Nice fire," she commented. After setting her purse on a small table, she walked to the L-shaped sofa and sat about midway of the longest side.

"Perfect night for a fire," Duke replied. He went over to the table with the tray. "Would you like a splash of brandy in your coffee?"

"A very small splash."

Duke prepared their cups, adding cream to hers.

"You remembered I use cream," she said with a faint smile, accepting the cup he handed her.

"I remember every word that was ever spoken between us," he said quietly, taking his own cup and sitting on the short side of the sofa so he could have the pleasure of looking at her.

"Not every word was pleasant," she said with a pointed little laugh caused by a sudden surge of discomfort. Had it really been necessary to be so sharp-tongued with him at the Lockland Grange, for instance?

He smiled. "Guess it wasn't." He sipped from his cup. "But I'm hoping that will change."

Her heart skipped a beat, but she bravely looked into his eyes. "Why, Duke?"

"Do you really have to ask?"

She looked down at the cup in her hands. "Maybe what I should be asking is what you want from me."

"Do you ask every man you date that question?"

A frown formed between her eyes. "No, but you're... different." Maybe she could make him understand how confused she was about their relationship, she thought.

He nodded with an expression that openly applauded her wisdom, though Lola missed it as she was looking, rather intently, at the cup in her hand. "I know what you mean," Duke said. "You're different for me, too."

Her eyes lifted. "Do... do I disturb you?" *As much as you disturb me?*

"In a hundred ways. I've never met a woman who disturbed me more."

She hurriedly answered, feeling that she could be making some headway. "That's exactly my point, Duke. Neither of us is comfortable with the other. Why are we dating at all?"

He leaned forward to hit her with a challenging look. "You're not at all dense, Lola. You know the answer to that question. Tell me you don't think about me when we're not together."

Headway, be damned. Unless she lied through her teeth, she was not going to win this debate. She sucked in a shaky breath. "Maybe we should be going. The storm..."

"Don't worry about the storm." Rising, Duke placed his cup on a table and then sat beside her. "You want to know where the real storm is? It's in here..." He tapped his chest. "...and in there." He touched her just below her left breast.

"Duke..." she said in a near whisper. This was the pass she'd known was coming, the reason why she had tried to make him more understanding of her equivocation. She also knew she should elude his next move by getting up from this sofa and putting space between them—while she still could.

And yet she sat there, breathed in his scent and permitted a sensual languor to spread throughout her system.

He was wearing a white shirt and black pants, both in the Western style, and looked so utterly handsome that she wanted to just sit there and stare at him. He had the ability to dull her common sense, she realized weakly when she made no objection to his taking the cup from her hand. He left her side only long enough to place the cup next to his on the table.

Then he was back, sitting closer this time, close enough that their thighs were pressed together. His arm slipped around her shoulders, and with his other hand he tilted her chin so that her head was cradled in the crook of his elbow.

He looked into her eyes for the longest time. Her heart was beating like a wild thing, because she was looking back into his eyes and seeing exactly what he was thinking in their dark and simmering depths. This was how he was answering her question about what he wanted from her, not with words but with actions.

A silent groan ripped through her mind. Heaven help her, it was what she wanted, too. However this unnerving relationship ended up, she couldn't resist his charisma. As though of its own volition, her left hand rose from her lap to the back of his neck.

He lowered his head and pressed a tender kiss to the corner of her mouth. Her breath caught, and she held it while his lips moved across hers to the other corner.

"I feel so much for you, Lola," he whispered, dropping kisses along her forehead. His breath on her hairline raised goose bumps on her skin. "Tell me you feel something for me, too."

"Even if I don't know what it is?" she asked, her own voice as whispery as his.

"Maybe at first no two people know exactly what's drawing them together." He kissed the tip of her nose. "Maybe it takes time. But I know one thing for certain. The minute I saw you, I felt . . ." He stopped, because the right word eluded him. What *was* the right word, anyway? He recalled feeling desire—Lola had instantly made him think of sex—but dare he speak so candidly?

"I felt something very special," he finally said, deciding that was a much safer way of expressing himself. "I think you did, too."

Her glance slipped sideways, avoiding his eyes. "I . . . I really don't want to talk about it."

Duke's eyes narrowed thoughtfully. She was in his arms but didn't want to talk about feelings. This was a unique situation for him. In his past experiences, women were the ones who wanted to discuss feelings, pressing him to do so, in fact. Now he was pressing Lola for a confession of affection, again, and she was backing off, again. Strange how the worm had turned.

"All right, we won't talk about it." He put his face in her hair and inhaled its clean, slightly perfumed scent. "Not tonight," he whispered, bringing her head to his chest.

His heartbeat was fast and hard, and she listened to it while her own pulse raced with the same frenzied rhythm. Being snuggled by strong, masculine arms felt very good. She brought her hand down from the back of his neck, letting it drift slowly down his shoulder and chest. The heat of his body came through his shirt and permeated her own hand. She shivered from the arousing sensation.

"You're not cold, are you?" he asked.

"No, I'm not cold," she whispered tremulously. What she was doing was sinking deeper and deeper into a seething cauldron of emotion that perversely seemed like an exquisite prize she must somehow attain.

"Lola . . ." He tilted her chin again, but this time he only looked into her eyes for a moment before pressing his mouth to hers. Her lips were immediately pliant under his, causing a roaring in his head, and it was only a matter of seconds before the kiss had evolved from tender to passionate. This was where she belonged, in his arms, in his home.

In his home? The thought was rife with staggering implications, and he broke the kiss to probe the depths of her eyes again. Was he falling in love with this beautiful, sensual woman? Thinking in the back of his mind of . . . of *marriage?* His heart had already been pounding, but now it felt as though it were trying to break through the wall of his chest.

He drew in an uneasy breath and forced his thoughts away from such serious subjects. Lola certainly wasn't ready to talk about them, and even hinting at either love or marriage was apt to destroy her mood, which he definitely did not want to do.

Laying his hand on the side of her face, he kissed her again. As kiss melted into kiss and his blood pressure soared, he slowly brought his hand down, caressing her throat, her shoulder and then her breasts through her clothing. He was rewarded with a husky whimper deep in her throat.

They both went a little crazy then, undoing each other's buttons, pushing clothing aside. Duke turned and lay back on the sofa, bringing her down on top of him. Spreading his legs, letting the right one dangle over the edge of the sofa, he molded her body to his, all the while kissing her... kissing her.

Her dress was open to the waist; he pushed it and her bra straps from her shoulders. She wriggled her arms free of the confining fabric, and her bare breasts, full and lush, were all but in his face. In the next second, that was exactly where they were, because he buried his face in her soft flesh, licking at first one nipple, then the other. Without even thinking about it, she slipped her shoes off and let them fall to the floor.

They were both breathing in pants and gasps, drowning out the rain and the music. But neither of them was listening, anyway. Lola wouldn't let herself be shocked by what was happening. She had never felt such a driving, demanding need before, not for anyone or anything. Whether it was right, wrong or somewhere in between really didn't matter; she wasn't going to stop either Duke or herself.

Her dress was in the way, she decided through the haze of desire clouding her mind. It was a problem easily remedied. Sitting up, she took hold of the skirt and yanked the garment over her head, carelessly tossing it on the floor. Undoing the clasp of her bra, she got rid of it, as well.

The dark and smoldering expression in Duke's eyes as he looked at her, naked except for lacy, black bikini panties and thigh-high hose, made her feel seductive and beautiful.

"You look as though you like what you're seeing," she said raggedly.

"Believe it, baby, believe it," he growled, pulling her down again to ravish her mouth with rough, feverish kisses. He felt as though he couldn't touch her enough, and his hands moved up and down her back and then into her panties to caress the sweet curves of her buttocks. "You are so damned beautiful," he whispered thickly.

"I might say the same about you if you weren't wearing so many clothes," she whispered back, teasing him with a kiss. "Are you beautiful, Duke? Show me."

He couldn't believe she'd said that. She was no shy little flower when it came to something she wanted, and apparently she wanted him. He'd known since they'd met that this would happen between them, but he hadn't dared to hope it would be tonight. Maybe she had suspected as much. Maybe that was the reason for her reaction to the Hansens' absence. One thing was certain: he couldn't read Lola's mind.

Or he hadn't been able to until now. Wherever their relationship went from here, she was his for tonight. It was on her face, in her eyes and the provocative curve of her lips. He couldn't have been more elated.

Rearing up, he slid his left leg under her and put both feet on the floor. Then he stood, bringing her with him, lifting her from the sofa and into his arms.

She hugged his neck and whispered, "Where are we going?"

"To my room." His strides were long and purposeful. He took the two stairs and headed for the bedroom wing.

Lola closed her eyes. She had never been carried to a man's bedroom before, and the sensation merely added fuel to the already blazing desire controlling her senses.

Pushing open a door with the toe of his boot, Duke entered a dark room, one of the few in the house, Lola thought when she opened her eyes. Maybe all the bedrooms were dark, she mused in a vague way, but the rest of the house had been lit up like a Christmas tree when they'd arrived.

Obviously Duke knew his bedroom well enough that he didn't need light, because he walked unerringly to his bed and laid her on it. Then he switched on the lamp next to it and started undressing.

Lola stared, all but holding her breath. Watching Duke undress was the most exciting event of her life. His chest was deep and furred between his nipples. His torso looked hard as rock, but she knew from her own touch that it was firm and muscled but not at all unyielding.

He kicked off his boots and sat on the edge of the bed to yank off his socks. Standing again, he faced her to open his pants and push them down, his briefs going at the same time. Lola gulped but didn't avert her eyes. She had told him to show her his beauty, and he wasn't a bit modest about doing so.

"You *are* beautiful," she whispered hoarsely, her gaze washing up and down his body.

He chuckled softly. "Let's get under the covers."

Lola shifted around on the bed so he could pull down the spread, lightweight blanket and top sheet. But he pulled them way down, nearly to the foot of the bed. Then he lay down beside her, supported his head on his elbow and looked at her. In her hose and panties, she was a temptress, the sexiest woman he'd ever seen.

His free hand rose to skim her waist, her hip, and then moved up to her breasts. He dipped his head, and his mouth found hers. Kissing him back, she inched closer to him until there was no room for his hand between her breasts and his chest. Relishing that sensation, he dropped his hand to the lacy top of her panties and began working them down.

"My stockings," she gasped between fiery kisses.

"Leave them on." With her panties gone, he parted her thighs for his hand. Locating the core of her passion, he rubbed very gently, very tenderly, and it was only minutes before she couldn't lie still.

Moaning and nearly weeping, she took matters into her own hands by removing *his* hand from between her legs and urging him on top of her. At the last second, a ray of common sense prevailed. "Do you have protection?" Her voice was rusty and sounding like a stranger's.

"Yes." He reached behind him to the bedside table and pulled out its top drawer, realizing that if she hadn't reminded him, he would have completely neglected protection. But he was in an agony of desire; maybe no excuse for such laxness, but somehow a reason for forgetting something he never had before.

He was out of reach for only a few seconds, but Lola suffered the most peculiar sensation; it was as though a part of herself had suddenly been cut away.

Before she could decipher its meaning, Duke was back, picking up exactly where he had left off. Kissing her hungrily, he slid into the heat of her body. Lola moaned softly as pleasure began spiraling through her system. But it wasn't the complete, fulfilling pleasure she had to have and knew would come. Her body strained to his, moving with his tempo, striving for that euphoric moment.

They reached it together. "Duke...oh, Duke," she cried, writhing beneath him.

He cried out, too. "Lola . . . Lola . . . baby."

And then there was silence. Sated and exhausted, Lola closed her eyes. She was barely aware of Duke's movements, though it seemed to her that she was alone in the bed for a few minutes. Then he was curled around her again, and she took a deeply satisfied breath and fell asleep.

"Lola?" Duke said softly. When she didn't answer, he raised his head to peer at her face. Lying back, he smiled and closed his own eyes. Right at that moment, everything seemed very right with the world.

He, too, fell asleep.

Eight

—

Lola came partially awake. With her eyes still closed, she lay unmoving and enjoyed a delirium of delicious feelings. Warmth seemed to be surrounding her, penetrating her very soul, and the bed beneath her relaxed and sated body felt as soft and cushy as the finest goose down.

The bed! Her eyes jerked open. The lamp was still on. Duke was wrapped around her, one arm thrown across her waist, and he was sleeping so soundly she could just barely detect his breathing. Her heart began pounding. Not from guilt or because of morals, but how wise was it for a woman to sleep with a man she wasn't sure of?

And what time was it? She hadn't worn a watch to Duke's house, and she craned her neck to see the clock on the stand on his side of the bed. Midnight! She had slept for hours. Groaning silently, she put her head back on the pillow. She had to wake Duke, and she would give almost anything to be able to slip from his bed unnoticed and get home on her own. Why, oh, why, hadn't she insisted on taking her own car? Why did she follow his direction, even while bearing that odd wariness of him? An even more disturbing question came next: why was she so uneasy with a man who was attractive enough to entice her into his bed and was, as Betty had told her, considered the best catch in the county?

Of course that could be merely Betty's opinion. But Lola's own opinion was that Duke seemed solidly placed and financially secure. He was exceptionally good-looking and—Lola felt her pulse flutter with enchanting memories—an incredible lover. So with all those pluses, why couldn't she get past the trepidation nagging at her and just let herself fall in love with him?

On the other hand, maybe she *was* falling in love with him. Certainly she had felt something lovely and unique for him while they were making love.

But he sometimes made the most perturbing remarks, such as that she should get rid of her store, and that she should never be there alone. They were possessive, overly protective remarks, sounding more like commands than suggestions. Obviously he was a man accustomed to issuing orders and having people jump to obey. Maybe that was what she had sensed from him all along, and why she couldn't completely relax and let nature takes its course. She was not, after all, a woman who took orders well.

It really was the chasm between them, she concluded with a frown, not particularly pleased that she had finally figured out the cause of her ambivalence with Duke. It was, after all, a point of serious conflict that wasn't apt to vanish just because things would go smoother without it.

Still frowning, Lola wished that tonight hadn't happened. Given Duke's nature and personality, he was bound to read more into it than she was willing to concede. Damn, she thought with no small amount of self-directed irritation. The drive back to town had every chance of being a discomfiting, unnerving trip.

Regardless, she had to get home. Turning slightly, she laid her hand on Duke's arm and shook it. "Duke?"

A sleepy "Hmm" was his response, along with a snuggling movement that aligned their bodies more perfectly. Lola silently mouthed another "damn," because she could

feel every inch of him touching some part of her, and it
wasn't even slightly unpleasant. In fact, she was too realis-
tic to tell herself that, even though she rued tonight, it was
never going to happen again. Flawless sexuality between a
man and a woman was too rare to be cast aside as trivial. It
was just that she didn't want any discussions about perma-
nency between them.

It was obvious that Duke had immediately returned to a
deep sleep, which had Lola picturing herself shaking him
good and hard to bring him awake.

But then she had a better idea. Very cautiously and slowly
she began easing toward the edge of the bed. Inching her
way and all but holding her breath, she slipped from under
Duke's arm. Moving silently and making sure she didn't
jostle the bed, she swung her feet around to the floor.

The first thing she noticed was her sagging hose. Leaving
the bed and standing, she finally took a normal breath and
bent over to pull up her stockings. Snags and runs appeared in both of them. "Great," she mumbled.

Moving around the foot of the bed without making a
sound, she finally found her panties, which she picked up
and carried with her to the living room. There, beside the
sofa, was her crumpled dress, her bra and her shoes. She
dressed with the speed of light, took her purse and entered
the guest bathroom.

"Oh, good Lord," she muttered at the disheveled reflection she saw in the mirror. Hastily she brushed her hair and
put on a light coating of lipstick. It helped; at least she
didn't look quite so much like the morning after.

Drawing a deep breath, she returned to Duke's bedroom.
For a moment she merely stood in the doorway and looked
at him. The bed was rumpled; a sheet was twisted around his
lower half, but not very effectively. Most of his behind and
long legs were in full view, and she couldn't help admiring
his physique.

Nor could she help remembering how ardently he'd made
love to her. Considerately, too, as though she hadn't been
just another notch on his bedpost.

But then she hadn't thought that he might be having ideas of that nature, had she? To the contrary, he had seemed to be staking a disturbingly permanent claim.

Oh, stop procrastinating, she told herself irately. *You have to wake him up and get yourself back to town.*

Approaching the bed, she gave it a shake and then backed away. "Duke?" Twice more she went through the exercise before he groggily turned over and looked at her.

Blinking, he finally registered her standing there, fully dressed and with a not too friendly expression. "Lola? What's going on?"

"What's going on is that I have to get home, and it's already after midnight. Please get up and get dressed."

"Uh, sure, but...how come you're already dressed? How long've you been awake?" He didn't like the chilly look in her eyes. After their incredible lovemaking, he should at least see a smile. A little warmth wouldn't be out of place, either.

"Please hurry," she said impatiently. "I'll wait in the living room." She walked out.

"Well, hell," Duke mumbled, wondering what was in her craw now. Scrambling off the bed, he gathered his clothes and began dressing. It was still raining, and he scowled about it. If this hard, pounding rain continued much longer, there would undoubtedly be some flooding to contend with. He would have to check the ranch's creeks and ponds first thing in the morning.

As he sat on the bed to pull on his boots, his thoughts returned to Lola, who had seemed almost angry with him. For certain she wasn't the same woman who had made love with him and then fallen asleep in his arms. Why had she withdrawn again? Why was she upset?

Finger-combing his hair, he got to his feet and headed for the living room. It was vacant, but he heard sounds from the kitchen. Changing directions, he called, "Lola?"

"In here," came from the kitchen.

He walked in and saw her closing the door of the dishwasher. "I put in our coffee cups and also rinsed out the coffeepot," Lola explained. "I don't know where that silver tray and decanter of brandy goes, so would you please put them away?'' She gestured to the items on the counter.

Duke folded his arms and slouched against the doorway with a cynical twist to his lips. ''What're you trying to do, erase every sign that you were even here tonight? Maybe you're thinking that without physical evidence, you can pretend it never happened.''

Not expecting a frontal attack, she gave him a surprised look. ''Do you have some kind of problem?''

''Since you asked, yes, I have a problem. Why didn't you wake me when you awoke? Why sneak out of bed the way you did?''

''I don't think I have to explain my every move to you,'' she said sharply. She couldn't deny sneaking out of bed when that was exactly what she'd done.

His eyes narrowed. ''You're angry and I want to know why.''

''Don't demand, Duke. You're very good at demanding, and I don't like it.''

''What in hell are you talking about?''

''You're also very good at seduction. Plying me with wine and brandy...''

''You think I planned the whole thing?'' His voice held some incredulity.

''Do you actually expect me to believe you didn't?'' Lola threw up her hands. ''Look, it's late and I want to go home.''

Duke was getting angry himself. Lola could try the patience of a saint, and no one knew better than he that patience wasn't one of his better traits.

''Fine. Let's go,'' he said gruffly, heading for the entry to retrieve their coats. She was right behind him, and he held her raincoat for her to slip into. She did so grudgingly, being careful not to let him touch her.

Duke left his jacket on the hook and pulled on a yellow rain slicker instead. He settled his hat on his head and looked at her. ''Guess you turn into a pumpkin at midnight, or into something. I can't begin to guess what brought on your present mood, but nothing you can say or do is going to change what happened here tonight."

She flushed. "Let's go."

Duke just gave her a dark look and opened the outside door.

They ran through the rain to his four-wheeler and got in. Duke started the engine. Lola hooked her seat belt. The windshield wipers came on. Neither said a word.

They were halfway to town before Duke broke the silence. "I don't understand you, Lola. I want to, very badly, but I can't seem to make the grade. Did I do something to make you angry?"

Yes, you made love to me! You're making me fall in love with you and I'm not sure I want to! "I'm not angry," she said tonelessly, staring straight ahead.

He took his eyes from the black, wet road long enough to send her a questioning glance. "If you're not angry, what are you? Please don't say regretful. We didn't do anything wrong. And I didn't ply you with liquor to get you to bed."

"I suppose you didn't make a pass, either," she said dryly.

"Yes, I made a pass. I did what I've been wanting to do since the day we met. But what did you do? Did you say 'No, Duke'? You kissed me back. You wanted exactly what I did. Lola, whatever else is going on in your mind, don't lie to yourself about that."

"Thanks loads for the advice," she said with heavy sarcasm. "That's another thing you're very good at, handing out advice that no one wants to hear."

"So, I'm good at making demands, seducing innocent women and handing out advice. Well, let me tell you what you're good at, lady. You're damned good with low blows."

"I never said I was innocent, so stop putting words in my mouth!"

"Maybe that was my word. Give me some credit, Lola. I'm not completely without intelligence."

"I wasn't innocent, which you have to know."

"You're confusing innocent with virginal, sweetheart. As tough as you try to act, there is an innocence about you.

And for God's sake, don't take that as an insult and do something to destroy it. It happens to be an extremely appealing part of your personality."

When she made no reply, he said, "Please don't be mad at me."

"I'm not mad at anyone. Except for myself," she said with a touch of bitterness.

"Because you made love with me?"

She lifted her chin, rather defiantly. "Because I made love with you when I knew beforehand that I should keep things cool between us."

"Why, for Pete's sake? What's wrong with you and I becoming lovers? Lola, you confound me."

"And you confound me," she shot back. "I really don't want to talk about it. In fact, we're not talking, we're arguing. As usual. We're always arguing about something, aren't we? Doesn't that tell you something? It tells me we're very different people with *very* different opinions and attitudes."

"We are *not* different!" Duke said gruffly. "That's what you can't seem to grasp, or refuse to admit. You might prefer thinking we're different from each other, but it's not true."

"Those remarks *prove* our differences," Lola snapped. "Your insistence that you and I are alike is ridiculous. Duke, do me a favor and just drop it, okay? I don't want to argue anymore. It's been a long, trying day and I'm exhausted."

"It wouldn't have been a trying day if you hadn't been alone in the store when that animal came in with a knife."

She cracked. "If you say that one more time, I...I swear I'll never speak to you again. Do I tell you how to run your ranch? No, and the reason I don't is that I have no idea how to manage a cattle operation. Fine. I accept that. What you have to accept is that you know nothing about a retail sales business. Nor do you have any right to tell me how to run my store. So just stay the hell out of it. Besides, that incident wasn't the only trying portion of the day, and I'm sure I don't have to spell it out for you to catch my meaning."

"You're talking about tonight."

She didn't answer, merely turned her head to stare blankly at the rain running down the side window.

Feeling frustrated because of her silence, Duke slapped the steering wheel. "I just don't get why tonight upset you so much." She still didn't answer. "I suppose you're not going to talk to me at all now."

"Change the subject and I might."

Duke's frustration magnified. Change the subject. Her attitude was infuriating, and it took teeth-gritting self-control to stop himself from telling her so. This relationship was going nowhere, and it was all her doing. She'd made love with him like there was no tomorrow, and now she was mad at him because of it. Damned woman. She was driving him crazy.

Well, he didn't need it. This was the end of the line. No more, he thought, glad to see the lights of Rocky Ford, dim and wavery in the heavy rainfall. He drove the shortest possible route to Charlie's Place and pulled into the driveway.

"Don't get out," Lola said.

"Don't worry, Lola, I wasn't going to," Duke said coldly.

Her eyes widened for a moment. He was mad as hell. Well, wasn't that just too bad?

Opening her door, she slid her feet to the ground. "Good night."

He said nothing. Seething and clenching his jaw, he waited until she had gone into the house, then he slammed the shifting lever into Reverse and backed up fast.

So, that's that, he thought. It's over and good riddance. What man needed what Lola dished out? He sure as hell didn't.

Inside, Lola turned off the lights Charlie had left on for her as she made her way through the house to her bedroom. She arranged her raincoat on a hanger and hooked it over the closet door so the drops of water on it wouldn't dampen her other clothes in the closet. A shower would feel wonderful right now, but she didn't want to wake Charlie so she yanked off her clothes, dropped a nightgown over her head, turned off her bedroom lights and crawled into bed.

Then she drew in a long, soulful breath and finally let herself think about the evening. To her chagrin, tears formed in her eyes and began dripping down her temples to the pillow. Why was she crying?

Oh, damn, *why* was she crying?

Rocky Ford's small-town newspaper came out three times a week. Sunday editions were its most widely read publication. The woman occupying room 116 bought a copy on her way into the Sundowner Motel's restaurant. After ordering breakfast, she sipped coffee and began perusing the news. She had previously learned that this particular paper contained mostly local news, which was why she liked it. One could pick up a great deal of information about a place and its inhabitants from a gossipy little newspaper.

Thus far she hadn't seen the Fanon name mentioned in any of the papers she'd read front to back, but there it was on today's front page, blazing at her in a black headline that said, "Lola Fanon Robbed At Knifepoint." Quickly she began devouring the article.

Lola Fanon, owner of the Men's Western Wear store on Ralston Street, was accosted late yesterday afternoon during a thunderstorm by a man with a knife who demanded all the money she had in the store. Miss Fanon gave the man the cash from the register, then somehow managed to escape to Herb's Diner next door to call the police. The man apparently left before the police arrived, but a suspect is in custody, due to the quick work of our able police department. It is this reporter's understanding that Miss Fanon will attempt to identify the man in custody sometime today.

Lola Fanon is the niece of Charlie Fanon, owner of Charlie's Place, a well-known establishment on Foxworth Street. Miss Fanon was not available for comment last night, but Mr. Fanon reports that his niece came through the ordeal without injury and is doing fine.

A robbery of this nature is rare in Rocky Ford. As the

facts of the episode unfold, this newspaper will keep its readers informed.

Lowering the paper, the woman sat back. Lola Fanon was Charlie's niece, which opened up a whole new avenue of thought. Did Charlie have other relatives? None bearing the Fanon name were listed in the local telephone directory, but perhaps they lived elsewhere.

Little by little she was learning things about Charles Fanon. She drew a nervous breath, wondering if she had learned enough yet to confront him.

She was still wondering about it, unhappily and with nothing resolved, when she left the restaurant and returned to her room.

With Officer Anderson at her side and two other men in the room, one of whom was the county prosecutor, Lola peered through a one-way window at a lineup of five men. "Don't worry, they can't see you," Anderson told her.

"I know the procedure," she said. It took only a quick glance at each man to pick the right one. "Number three."

Gary glanced at the two men with them and said with satisfaction, "Positive ID on Griff Lowell. We'll book him on armed robbery." He spoke into a telephone to the officer in the lineup room. "Hold number three."

Then he turned to Lola. "Please sit down."

There was a table with chairs around it, and Lola chose one and sat down.

"Miss Fanon, I'm Harold Cummings, the county prosecutor," the oldest man in the room said. "With your identification of Lowell, we have every possibility of putting him away for a good many years. If we ever get the chance, that is. You see, Officer Anderson obtained information through the FBI computer network and Lowell is wanted in three states for other crimes."

Officer Anderson spoke up. "You were very lucky yesterday, Miss Fanon. Lowell's other crimes include rape and murder."

Lola's hand rose to her throat. "Rape and murder?" she whispered. *Oh my God. I really could have been killed.*

Cummings took charge again. "Lowell is going to be released to the state of Maryland, Miss Fanon, where he'll be tried for murder. There are two other states ahead of us after Maryland. The point I'm trying to make is that we won't be bringing Lowell to trial anytime in the near future. In fact, we probably never will." He smiled. "His crime here is pretty low on the totem pole."

"Yes," she said, her voice cracking. "Uh, if I may ask, with so many other states after him, and with very little chance of Montana ever prosecuting him, why was it necessary that I identify him?"

"Matter of record, Miss Fanon," Cummings answered. "And if, for some unimaginable reason, Lowell should manage to escape penalty in those other states, we'll be prepared to prosecute. Thank you for coming in."

Shakily, Lola got to her feet. "You're...welcome."

Office Anderson escorted her from the room and to the front door of the building. "Goodbye, Miss Fanon."

"Goodbye." Lola started down the street to her parked car. It all seemed so unbelievable. Lowell was probably never going to be prosecuted for what he'd put her through yesterday.

Lost in a tangle of very disturbing thoughts, Lola didn't notice Duke leaning against the front fender of her car until she was only a few feet away. When she did see him, she felt an overwhelming urge to run into his arms. As overbearing as he could be, he represented the good things of life. People like Griff Lowell didn't exist in his world. And she didn't want them existing in hers, either.

But instead of running into Duke's arms, she slowed her pace and approached him cautiously.

At the sight of her pale, stricken face, Duke straightened. "Are you all right?"

"I...honestly don't know." Her voice was hoarse from the confusion tearing her apart.

"What happened in there?"

She told him, quickly and in the briefest possible terms. Duke looked as stunned as she felt. Then it occurred to her to wonder why he was here.

"Were you waiting for me?" she asked.

He was silent for a long moment, just looking at her. Finally he answered. "We have to talk. Not argue, talk." He'd hardly slept last night. Sometime in the night the rain had stopped, and today there was a pale sun in a still cloudy sky. He had checked the creeks and ponds on the ranch, and the flooding was only minimal, but nothing had seemed to matter except to see Lola again, in spite of his vows last night to stay away from her.

Looking away from the intensity of his eyes, she bit her lip. That startling session in the police department still had her quaking in her shoes. "Not now, Duke. I...I'm just not up to it."

"When, then? This afternoon? This evening?"

She took a deep, unsteady breath. "I don't know. Call later today. Maybe I'll be more myself in a few hours."

He reached for her hand and she let him hold it. "Why don't you come for a ride with me? I won't pressure you, I promise. A ride in the country might calm your nerves."

She gave her head a small shake. "Thank you, but I really need to go home."

"You can't deal with me right now, can you?"

Her eyes rose to meet his. "Maybe that's true. All I know for sure is that I need to be alone for a while." And maybe talk to Charlie, she added to herself.

Duke finally nodded. "All right. I'll call this afternoon." He wanted to pull her into his arms, to offer comfort, to convey his feelings, to hold her. Instead, he inhaled deeply and let go of her hand.

Then he walked around her car and opened the driver's door. When she was settled behind the wheel, he said quietly, "Talk to you later."

She nodded. "Yes, later. Goodbye."

He stood near the curb and watched her drive off, his heart beating a mile a minute.

Trouble or not, stubborn or not, Lola was the woman he was going to marry. He knew it now, as clearly and distinctly as he knew anything.

Nine

The woman in the blue sedan had watched Charlie and Lola come out of the house together. Lola had gotten into her car, Charlie into his pickup truck, and they had both driven away, going in different directions.

She had started her own car and followed Charlie's truck at a discreet distance. He didn't go far... only about ten blocks. The woman's eyes widened when she saw his destination, a little white church with a picture-pretty steeple. Charlie found a parking place on the street right away and she had no choice but to drive past him, as there wasn't another empty space in the entire block.

It was the closest she had thus far gotten to Charles Fanon, and she couldn't resist a look in his direction as she cruised by. He was just climbing out of his truck, and he gave her a friendly wave, as though they were old acquaintances.

Her stomach had lurched. He was a pleasant-looking man, she'd realized. And pleasant acting, as well. Like maybe he thought of everyone as his friend. It wasn't what

*she had expected from Charles A. Fanon and it was fresh
fodder for thought. At the very least, it was something to
add to the list of information she had been mentally com-
piling about the Fanon family.*

*In the next block, just beyond the church, was an empty
space at the curb. On impulse she maneuvered the blue sedan into the space, then wondered if she had the nerve to
actually walk into that church. Looking back through the
rear window, she could see a man standing at the open front
doors greeting parishioners; the minister, obviously.*

*Apparently Charlie had gone in while she was parking,
because he was nowhere in sight. She drew an unsteady
breath and waited. When the minister closed the doors, she
got out and slowly approached the church.*

*Then, gathering her courage, she put her hand on the
knob and turned it, opening the door a crack. A hymn was
starting, an old one that she knew. As silently as possible,
she went in, closed the door and slipped into the back pew.
The congregation was standing, singing the hymn.*

*It wasn't until the hymn was over and everyone was seated
that she located Charlie in the crowd.*

Drawing a quiet breath, she stared at the back of his head.

A block from the police station Lola changed her mind
about going directly home, and drove instead to her store.
As Ralston Street was all but vacant—normal on Sunday—
she parked at the curb in front of her business. Unlocking
the front door of the store, she went in, then stood in the silence and glanced around. She then turned and quickly
locked the door behind her.

It seemed different, she had to admit. Would she ever feel
completely secure in here again? How simple it was for
someone to walk in and . . .

No, she couldn't start thinking that way. Yesterday's oc-
currence would probably never happen again. And she
shouldn't be upset because Lowell wasn't going to stand trial
in Montana. Most people would be elated over not having
to endure such an ordeal.

But it didn't feel right. Lowell was probably never going to pay specifically for threatening her with a vicious-looking knife, and it didn't seem fair or just.

Sighing, Lola wandered over to the counter and cash register. All the register contained was coins, and she gave the drawer a push to close it. Then she went to her office and sat at her desk. Picking up a pencil, she began doodling on a yellow pad.

There was always some kind of work to do in the store, but she felt so aimless. So unsettled. Part of it had to do with the robbery and its startling aftermath this morning, but most of her unease was because of Duke, she realized after a few minutes of drawing circles and squiggles.

Her mind flashed to that moment on the sidewalk when she had seen him waiting for her and had instantly wanted to walk into his arms. Her next thoughts were of last night, of his lovemaking, his body, his kisses. She dragged in a deep breath as the erotic images of the two of them, naked in his bed, paraded through her brain. The simple—or very complex—truth was that she wanted him again. Her pulse fluttered and a flame ignited in the pit of her stomach. Was she falling in love with Duke or just having hot flashes because she was so sexually attracted to him?

If handled discreetly, they could have an *affaire d'amour* without too much gossip. People would speculate, of course. Charlie would wonder where their relationship was going, and he might even ask. But some couples dated for years and it was pretty safe to assume they weren't playing tiddledywinks every time they were together. It was no secret that Duke already had conducted a long-term relationship with a woman named Tess Hunnicutt, and no one seemed to think badly of him for it. An affair was really the only answer when two people were enormously attracted to each other but unsure of a lifetime commitment.

In a sudden burst of impatience, Lola threw down her pencil. *Why* was she unsure? Dammit, she had never been one of those people who didn't know their own mind and couldn't make a decision if their life depended on it. She had never had any trouble at all with decisions.

But then, she'd never been faced with decisions about a man who made her feel so jagged and on edge, had she?

After talking to Lola, Duke drove to a friend's house on the outskirts of town. He planned to visit with Darrin Shanks for an hour or so, then make that call to Lola. But Darrin, his wife and two kids were getting ready for a family outing. Not wanting to intrude on their plans, Duke stayed only a few minutes. Driving away, he thought of any number of other people he could drop in on, but his heart wasn't really set on socializing, so he decided to just knock around on his own for a while.

He stopped at a small café for a cup of coffee, killing about twenty minutes. Back in his rig, he decided to drive out to Holden's car lot to see what was for sale. Holden's was on the other side of Rocky Ford, and the shortest route to the car lot was a direct cut through town; it was pure coincidence that Duke chose to take Ralston Street.

Only a few cars were parked along Ralston, so he couldn't possibly miss seeing Lola's vehicle parked in front of her store. So, he thought, she hadn't gone home after all. She was in the store doing—what? Worrying? Working? Reliving yesterday's frightening event? Thinking about last night with him?

Pulling up behind her car, he sat there with the motor idling, weighing the pros and cons of interrupting whatever it was that Lola was doing in there all by herself. His stomach tensed as an idea came to mind: it was entirely possible that she'd come here instead of going home to avoid his call. Even though it had been her suggestion that he call her later.

His jaw set at a stubborn angle as he turned off the ignition; this was as good a place to talk as any other. Getting out, he crossed the sidewalk and peered through one of the plate glass windows. Lola was nowhere to be seen.

Moving to the door, he pounded on the metal frame with his fist, figuring that she wouldn't hear a quieter knock if she was in the back of the building.

At her desk, Lola raised her head, uncertain of what she'd just heard. But in a few seconds the staccato beats were repeated, and she got up to investigate. The second she was in the doorway of her office, she saw Duke at the front door.

"Oh," she whispered, shaken suddenly. Thinking the word *affair* and actually discussing it, or giving enough hints for him to get the message, were worlds apart. At the same time, just seeing him was raising her blood pressure. He affected her as no man ever had, and she had to deal with it . . . in some way.

Traversing the store with its racks and tables of merchandise, she reached the front door, unlocked and opened it.

"I thought you'd probably gone home," she said by way of a greeting.

"That's what I thought about you, too," he returned, stepping inside.

Lola immediately relocked the door, then turned to face him. "Well..." Without warning, words escaped her. He'd said they needed to talk, and she herself had been thinking along those lines only minutes ago. It was just that his list of topics and hers could be miles apart. And besides, like it or not, his very presence was daunting. He was too good-looking and he did something peculiar to her nervous system. For instance, she felt as if her lungs weren't getting enough air. An aversion to letting him know how breathless he made her feel had her nearly choking.

"Well?" he echoed, his hands on his hips and his eyes never straying from hers.

"Umm..." She *had* to have air, and she gave the whole thing away by sucking in a huge breath. The change in his expression, the understanding, set her heart to hammering.

He took a step forward, but before he could touch her she spun away. "We can talk in my office," she mumbled. If anything even remotely sexual was going to happen between them, it wasn't going to occur in front of her windows so any passerby could chuckle over it.

Duke followed her rapid retreat, his gaze on the exciting way her skirt rippled and flowed because of the swaying movement of her hips. She might think like a man, but there was nothing physically manly about Lola Fanon. In fact, she was the most flagrantly feminine woman he'd ever known. Seductively feminine. Intriguingly feminine.

In her office, she gestured at a chair. "Sit down, if you'd like."

"I don't think so," he said softly, advancing on her.

She watched him coming nearer. "I thought you wanted to talk."

"I did. I do. But first things first. You've really got me going, sweetheart," he said huskily as he pulled her into his arms.

She didn't even attempt to stop him. This was what she wanted, too, to be pressed against him, to feel his heat and desire, to acknowledge her own. An affair, yes. It made better sense the more she thought about it. She put her arms around his neck and tilted her head to look into his eyes.

"Lola," he whispered, and then took her lips in a kiss of raw hunger. She kissed him back in the same feverish way, and by the third kiss they were tearing at each other's clothing.

Duke pushed her up against a wall. In seconds her panties were gone, his jeans were unzipped and sagging, and he was inside her. Gasping and perspiring, she clung to him and matched the thrusts of his body with her own. The sounds he made were guttural and almost savage. Occasionally she heard her name. Occasionally she said his name. But mostly there was only the hoarse moans and whimpers of a pleasure so consuming that Lola couldn't think, let alone speak.

She wound one leg around his, balancing precariously on the tips of her other toes. Then he lifted her higher and she couldn't touch the floor at all. With both of her legs wrapped around him, he carried her to her desk and laid her down. She recognized the pad she'd been doodling on under her back, but it was a trivial discomfort and barely noticed.

Duke's kisses fell on every inch of her face and throat. But then kisses were forgotten, because their passion had reached the explosive stage. Riding her hard and fast, he heard her cry out. His own roaring release came a second later.

He fell across her, utterly drained.

Minutes later he raised his head. Her eyes fluttered open; Lola and Duke looked at each other. His spirit soared when he saw a smile slowly take shape on her lips.

"Lola, let's get ma—" Her fingers on his mouth stopped him.

"I need to get up," she said. "You didn't use protection."

"Oh, hell," he muttered, backing away then helping her up and off the desk. As she dashed for the bathroom, he shook his head. How in hell could he have forgotten protection? He'd come close to doing the same thing last night. Making love to Lola apparently depleted his normal common sense. If she had gotten pregnant today...?

A grin suddenly broke out on his face. The idea of Lola having his baby was thrilling. His own thoughts amazed him. Talk about a man doing some major changing! Since meeting Lola he'd gone from a dyed-in-the-wool bachelor to a guy with a silly grin at the mere thought of fatherhood.

But then his elation shrank some. He'd nearly proposed, and she had stopped him before he could finish. She had to have known what he'd been trying to say, and she'd deliberately stopped him. So, he thought, his eyes narrowing in speculation, she didn't want to talk about marriage. Maybe he was moving too fast. Their relationship was pretty darned new, after all. It was funny how a man could be completely contented with single life one day and then walk into a store and fall head over heels for a woman. Guess that was how it happened, though.

At any rate, he wouldn't mention marriage again today.

In the little bathroom, Lola was thinking about the *M* word, as well. My Lord, when she walked out of this room, was Duke going to make another stab at proposing? She had to let him know, without hurting his feelings and destroying what they had, that she wasn't ready for marriage. How best to pull that one off, when he was so obviously getting serious and she... well, what *was* happening to her?

If she was falling in love with Duke, why not discuss marriage? She shivered as icy fingers suddenly walked up her spine. If the word *marriage* was actually spoken between them, everything would change.

But so would everything change if the word *affair* entered their vocabulary.

"Damn, damn, damn," she mumbled under her breath. It was a play-it-by-ear situation with Duke. Somehow she had to avoid serious conversations. Maybe that would change in time, maybe it wouldn't. But she had this knot of apprehension where Duke was concerned, even though she wanted him in her life.

Sighing dramatically, Lola finally left the bathroom and returned to her office. Duke was perched on the edge of the desk; he had put his jeans back on. When she came in, he got up.

His smile was warm, his eyes glowing, seemingly lit by inner fires. She had her own inner fires and couldn't deny them.

"Hi," he said softly, moving toward her. "Everything okay?" He put his arms around her, locking his hands behind her waist, then leaning back so he could see her face.

"We have to be more careful in the future," Lola murmured.

It was the first time she had suggested they *had* a future, and it touched Duke's soul. He drew her close and cradled her head against his chest.

"It's my responsibility," he said huskily. "I'll take care of it from now on, I promise." Right now, with her being so sweet and loving, he would promise her anything. His thinking of babies was foolish and premature; a shotgun wedding wasn't the best way to start their life together.

He kissed the top of her head, wishing he dared to confess his feelings for her and his hopes for the two of them. Very soon, he told himself, resigned to skipping that unique pleasure for the time being.

Pushing back to look at her, he said, "How about coming out to the ranch and seeing it in the light of day?"

"Why…yes. That's a wonderful idea. I really would like to see your ranch in daylight. But I have to run home for about an hour. I need to tell Charlie what happened at the police station, and I'd like to—" she smiled, reminding him of what had occurred on her desk "—shower and change clothes."

He smiled in return. "You're what's wonderful. I've got an idea. Wear some jeans and we'll take a horseback ride."

"Oh, really? Duke, I'm not sure about that. I've never made friends with horses."

He laughed and hugged her. "Then it's time you did. Any girl of mine *has* to be on speaking terms with horses."

It was decided that Duke would go on to the ranch and Lola would drive her own car there in about an hour. She drove home thinking about Duke's "girl of mine" remark. The more involved they became, the more possessive he got. It wasn't that he'd said it, it was that he really believed she was his girl now.

In a way she was, of course. There certainly wasn't any other man in her life. But neither did she like being considered a possession.

It was an enormous relief that Duke hadn't attempted another marriage proposal. Maybe he'd grasped her negativity on that subject when she had stopped him from completing that startling sentence. She hoped so. She hoped that he wasn't setting her up for another attempt at the ranch. It could be a very pleasant afternoon . . . if she could just be clever enough to sidestep serious conversations. Surely she could manage that, couldn't she?

Arriving home, she pulled into the driveway and got out of her car. Charlie's truck was there, so he was back from church. She'd been going with him since returning to Montana, actually just picking up where she'd left off years before. Charlie had insisted his kids attend Sunday school as youngsters, and church services when they were older. He didn't have to insist anymore; Lola truly enjoyed Sunday morning services, and she liked the pastor and his wife.

Rounding the house, Lola saw Charlie trimming the hedges. "Hi," she called.

Charlie turned. "Hi, honey. How'd it go?"

"Not like I expected." Lola walked over to him and told him about her session in the police department, omitting nothing.

"Murder and rape?" Charlie said with a deeply concerned frown.

Lola knew what he was thinking. "Don't dwell on it, Charlie," she said gently. "I know what could have happened, but it didn't. We all have to put it behind us."

After a moment, he nodded. "You're right. But I have the feeling there was an angel on your shoulder yesterday, honey."

Lola smiled. "I couldn't agree more. I'm going in now to change clothes, Charlie. Duke came by the police station and asked me to drive out and see his ranch in daylight. Should be interesting."

A smile broke out on Charlie's face. "Appears to me there's a lot that's interesting between you and Duke. Getting more interesting by the day, in fact."

She couldn't quite meet his eyes. He knew her so well, and there were aspects of her and Duke's relationship that she didn't want Charlie to figure out. "I guess that's true," she murmured. "Anyway, I'll probably be gone all afternoon."

"Enjoy yourself, honey. You're only young once."

"See you later." Lola walked away, heading for the stairs leading to the back door. Going into the house, she heard the phone ringing. She picked up the kitchen extension. "Hello?"

"Lola? This is Serena."

"Serena! Oh, it's good to hear your voice. How are you?"

"Great. Fabulous. Wonderful. I'm glad you answered. I want to talk to Dad, of course, but I also wanted to talk to you. Lola, I've met the most incredible man, and—" she gave a merry little laugh "—I'm in love!"

"Serena, that's wonderful. I'm so happy for you. Who is he? Tell me all about him."

"Well, he's handsome and intelligent and witty and..." She laughed again. "Actually, he's just about perfect, Lola.

His name is Edward Redding, and he works at the Pentagon. Like Ron, he can't talk about what he's doing. Edward won't even let me meet his coworkers. Everything's all secret and hush-hush, you know. But he's the most exciting man I've ever met. I'm walking on air these days.''

"Sounds like it.'' For a moment, Lola bit her lip. This was what love should be like, not the on-again, off-again feelings she had for Duke. Serena *knew* she was in love. What a marvelous thing that must be. No wonder she felt as though she were walking on air.

Now, *her* feet seemed solidly planted on the ground. If love made a woman feel weightless, then she was not in love with Duke. On the other hand, all he had to do to melt her bones was touch her. What did *that* mean?

"Is Edward a good lover?'' Lola asked.

Serena laughed. "I knew if anyone dared to ask that question, it would be you. Yes, cousin of mine, he's an incredible lover. Oh, Lola, I'd love to be able to spend a day with you. We always had such fun talking and giggling, didn't we?''

"Always, Serena.''

"Well, tell me about you. How's the store going?''

"The store is doing great.'' There was no reason to mention the robbery. It was in the past and she was going to forget it.

"And have you met anyone important? Are *you* walking on air, too?'' Serena asked in a teasing vein.

"Well...I've met someone, but I'm not walking on air.''

"Then he's not the right guy for you. I know the difference now, Lola. Oh, Lord, I just sounded so smug, didn't I? It's just that I'm so happy. I've never been so happy, Lola.''

"Sounds like you'll be staying in Washington after graduation.''

"Oh, yes. I wouldn't leave Edward for anything. That's what I want to talk to Dad about. I know he's been hoping I would set up a law practice in Rocky Ford. But he'll understand, don't you think?''

"I'm sure he will," Lola said, knowing that if Charlie was disappointed about Serena not coming home after graduation, he would still be happy for her.

"Maybe you'd better put him on the phone. He is home, isn't he?"

"He's outside working in the yard. I'll call him. Serena, I'm really thrilled for you. Let's talk again soon."

"Yes, let's."

"I'll get Charlie now. Bye." Laying the phone on the table, Serena hurried to the door. "Charlie? Serena's on the phone."

"Serena is? Well, now, isn't that nice?" Dropping his trimming shears, Charlie hastened to the house.

While he picked up the phone and began talking to his daughter, Lola went to her bedroom for clean clothes then continued on to the bathroom. Quickly she showered and got dressed.

All the while, she told herself that she was *not* jealous of Serena's happiness. She was happy for Serena, happy and thrilled.

Someday it would happen to her.

She stopped with a tear in her eye. Why couldn't it happen with Duke? What really was preventing her from walking on air?

Ten

Charlie was outside again when Lola was ready to go. Dressed in jeans, a white-and-blue striped shirt with long sleeves and boots with heels—which she figured might or might not be suitable for horseback riding but certainly were chic—she walked over to where he was working to say goodbye. "I'm leaving now, Charlie."

He looked up. "Have fun, honey."

There was a shadow in his eyes, and Lola knew he was disappointed about Serena's plans to stay in Washington. Anything that hurt Charlie hurt her, and yet she couldn't fault Serena for falling in love. This was one of those times when fateful circumstances tore loving family members apart. It was life.

Lola wanted to cheer Charlie up, to get his mind off Serena, so she laughed, albeit wryly. "I'm not sure about the fun, Charlie. Duke said he wants to put me on a horse. Can't you just picture me hanging on for dear life, scared witless?"

Charlie chuckled, making her feel better. "Nope. Can't

picture you scared witless about anything, honey. Get on that horse and enjoy it. I'm sure Duke wouldn't put you on anything but a gentle animal. You'll probably like horseback riding.''

"Well . . . we'll see,'' Lola said skeptically. She glanced at the sky. "It looks like it could rain again."

Charlie nodded. "Could be."

Lola put her arms around her uncle then and kissed his cheek. "Please don't be sad about Serena. She's so happy."

"I know, honey, I know." Charlie patted Lola's arm. "Don't worry about me. Go and enjoy yourself. The Burnhams invited me over for dinner, so I'm just puttering till it's time to go myself."

"All right," Lola said, keeping the wistfulness she was feeling from entering her voice. "See you later."

She was glad Charlie had something to do today. The Burnhams were old friends and she knew that he enjoyed seeing them. But, driving away, she let poignancy overtake her. Memories of the family before everyone went their separate ways flitted through her mind. Charlie had always been happiest when they were all together. Would all of them ever be together again? None of them knew when Ron might get a furlough. He'd been in Germany for over a year, and they knew his son only through snapshots and photographs. Actually, they knew his wife Candace better than Ron these days, as she did the letter writing. She wrote lovely long letters, always apologizing for Ron's being too busy to write himself. And he was gone a great deal. Candace often mentioned Ron's being away for ten days or two weeks, though even she wasn't permitted to know his destination or what he was doing.

Every time a letter arrived with that sort of message, Lola wondered if Ron's duty wasn't putting a strain on his marriage. Not that Candace ever hinted in that direction. But she was often alone in a foreign country with a small child. They had friends, of course, but a friend wasn't a husband, and Candace had to miss Ron terribly when he was gone for weeks at a time.

Well, she could worry about it, but it really was none of her business, Lola thought with a sigh. Neither was Serena's decision to live in Washington, D.C. But wasn't it strange that Charlie's own children were so far away and his niece was the one who had returned to Rocky Ford? He'd been so glad to see her, she recalled, so glad to hear that she was here to stay.

He was just the best person there ever was, she thought with a sudden touch of fierceness. His wife, Serena and Ron's mother, had died when they were mere toddlers. They had lived in California at the time, and Charlie had packed up his belongings and youngsters and moved to Montana. Lola figured that he'd moved his family to avoid unhappy reminders. Losing his wife at such a young age had to have been very traumatic for him. He had never remarried, which seemed truly romantic to Lola, and he had dedicated himself to giving his children—and ultimately her—the best life possible.

In Lola's estimation he had definitely succeeded. All three of them, Ron, Serena and herself, had turned out well. They had grown up saturated with Charlie's standards—basic decency, honesty, ambition and generosity. They had been deeply, openly loved and had known they could go to Charlie with anything, whether it be a problem to overcome or pride in an accomplishment. He had always been there for them, and—Lola smiled with the special softness she had always reserved for her uncle—he still was.

Lola's mind had been so full she was startled to see that she had reached Duke's long driveway. Turning into it, she stopped the car to do just a little more thinking—this time about Duke. His infractions were losing importance, she realized with a small frown. The more time she spent with him, the more her feelings grew for him. Maybe Serena's ardent declarations of love for her Edward were influencing her attitude toward Duke, but was possessiveness really such an intolerable trait? Duke was thinking of marriage, and...

Lola suddenly couldn't seem to catch her breath. Marriage. Maybe it wasn't Duke at all but the idea of total commitment that bothered her. Was that it? She'd been such a free spirit for so long that maybe she couldn't deal with forgoing even a portion of her independence.

But surely Duke wouldn't ask her to give up her independence, would he?

She answered that question in her very next heartbeat: Duke wouldn't ask, he would demand!

Okay, if she knew that about him, why was she putty in his hands when it came to sex?

"Chemistry," she groaned aloud. However else they did or did not mesh, there was too much chemistry between them to ignore. She loved making love with him. She was, in fact, already addicted to making love with him. Just thinking about what had happened in her office this morning gave her a tingling desire to experience it again.

Drawing in a long, slow breath, she stepped lightly on the gas pedal and got the car moving again. Coming out here to see his ranch was an excuse to see him. Yes, she had a certain amount of curiosity about the ranch, but a yearning to feel his mouth and hands on her again was much stronger.

Duke saw her coming from a front window of the house, and his blood began running faster. At the same time he noticed the sprinkles of rain on the window glass; he would still be able to show her the ranch, but not from horseback.

Watching her car getting closer, he gave his fantasies free rein. Someday Lola was going to live here as his wife, and if he stood at a window and watched her, as he was doing now, she would be coming home.

Where would she be coming from? Maybe she had attended a PTA meeting, or done some grocery shopping. This old house had been childless for much too long. He would like to fill it with the sounds of children, at least two, though if Lola agreed he would welcome more.

He shook his head, because he kept amazing himself with fantasies of children. Lola's babies. Lola. Beautiful, sensual Lola. God, he really had it bad for her.

When she parked her car next to his four-wheeler, he went outside to greet her. The rain was still only gentle little sprinkles, but he opened her door with a "Hi," took her hand and hurried her into the house.

"We won't be riding today," he told her, once inside.

"It's not raining very hard."

"I know, but it could get worse. We'll wait for a sunny day to get you on a horse."

She shrugged. "Fine with me." Her eyes met his. "I'm sure we can find...something else to do."

They stood there looking at each other. Duke dampened his lips with his tongue. "I could show you the ranch from my four-wheeler. It's capable of covering most of the terrain."

"That's one idea, I suppose," she said in a husky voice.

Her eyes were saying what her lips were not, and he was getting the message loud and clear. Closing the gap between them with two steps, he pulled her into his arms.

"Is this a better idea?" he whispered, pressing his mouth into her hair.

"I have to admit that it's the one I had in mind," she whispered back, wrapping her arms around his waist and moving her body against his. A sigh rippled through her. Nothing had ever felt so good as being in Duke's arms did. If sexual addiction to a man was love, then she was in love with him.

But she wasn't positive the two forces were even related, let alone synonymous.

"Are we alone in the house?" she whispered.

"Really alone. There's no one else anywhere on the ranch today. We don't work on Sundays—except sometimes during winter when we have to feed the cattle because of too much snow and ice—so everyone scatters on Sundays."

"Lovely," she murmured, snuggling closer. Her imagination went into overdrive. They could make love anywhere in this big house, and she knew exactly where she wanted to begin. "Do you have a fire in the living room fireplace?"

"As a matter of fact, yes." He tilted his head to see her face. "Why?"

"Take a wild guess."

He studied the sensual depths of her eyes for a moment, then nodded. "Let's go."

Arm in arm they walked to the living room. In front of the fireplace, watching each other, they began to undress. Internal pressures developed as their clothing fell away, piece by piece. Undressing started out at a reasonable speed, but before they were finished, it was as though they were running a race to see who could get naked first.

Duke won. Completely nude, he moved a large, plush area rug over to the fireplace and then sat down on it. Lola slid her panties down her legs and stepped out of them, her last garment, then went to join Duke on the rug.

He remained in a sitting position and pulled her down to straddle his lap. Face-to-face, they smiled at each other. But then they started kissing and touching and smiles were forgotten.

This time he remembered protection and managed to take care of it with only a minimal interruption. He entered her at once, drawing her so close that they were wound together as tightly as strands in a ball of yarn.

But such intimacy didn't promote stillness, and each began to move in some way. Duke's hands glided up and down her back, into her hair, grazing her thighs, her arms. She took his face between her hands and kissed his lips, breathily sliding her tongue into his mouth. He moved his hips slightly, only enough to cause a delicious friction where it counted the most.

Then he pushed her upper body back a little, and kissed a feverish path from her mouth to her breasts.

"You are so beautiful," he whispered raggedly before taking a nipple into his mouth and sucking gently. He brought his hands around to her breasts and lavished them with ardent caresses. Her head fell back, and she moaned deep in her throat. Her moan changed to a whimpering need when his hand slid down her belly and found the core of her desire.

"Oh, Duke," she whispered drunkenly as he played in the most artful, erotic way possible.

"Tell me it's good for you," he said thickly.

"It's good. You know it is," she gasped. She sought his lips for a wildly passionate kiss, then adjusted the arrangement of her legs so she could support herself on her knees. In this position, their hips were able to move more freely. They were both getting a little crazy, their eyes glazed, their breath coming in pants. He was still playing between her legs, and moving in and out of her. They stole quick, hot kisses from the other. One second her arms would be around his neck so tightly he couldn't move his head, and the next she was nipping at his lips, all the while maintaining a rhythm of their lower bodies that was gradually becoming frenetic.

Lola felt the final rush getting very close, and she began to cry out. "Duke...Duke..."

He heard and understood, and in one fluid movement he tipped her over to lie on her back, drew her legs up snugly around his waist, burrowed his hands beneath her hips and lifted her for the final ride to that one perfect moment.

In two minutes flat they reached it together, loudly, emotionally. Tears spilled from Lola's eyes. Duke fell forward on her, wondering if he'd ever have the strength to move anything again. Lola had the power to drain him as no woman ever had.

But then he knew he would move again, because they had made love this morning and he'd moved beautifully this afternoon. He took a satisfied breath. Give him an hour or so—maybe even less, given Lola's irresistible potency—and he'd be ready for action again.

In the meantime they could talk. Delighted with that thought, he lifted his head and smiled. The tears in Lola's eyes surprised him.

"Hey, are you okay?" he asked with some alarm.

She wiped her eyes. "Yes, I'm fine."

Relieved, he kissed her lips. "That was perfect, wasn't it?" he whispered.

"Perfect," she echoed.

He kissed her again, softly, tenderly, then looked at her with all the love in his soul. "I'm going to get up for a minute. Don't go away."

Her gaze slid from the intensity of his. "I won't."

When he had left her, she sat up and stared into the fire. Noticing that it had died down, she got up and put a log from the supply in a nook in the fireplace on the grate. It sparked and flamed almost instantly.

"Lovely wood," she murmured absently. Then she glanced around and whispered, "Lovely room." She could have this beautiful home. She could have Duke and his ranch and be in his bed every night.

Her chest seemed to tighten; was she in love with Duke or wasn't she? Was she losing her mind, or what? How could she do the things she did with Duke if she didn't love him? Never had she been promiscuous or easy; with Duke she was both. Whether or not the word *affair* ever passed between them, it was appropriate to what was happening.

The problem was, Duke thought otherwise. When he came back, he was apt to start talking about marriage.

Lola swallowed with a sudden surge of nervousness. But in the next instant her courage and confidence regrouped. She would not be talked or pressured into anything. Duke must accept her as she was or not at all.

That "not at all" idea gave her a shiver. Spotting an afghan on a chair, she darted over to get it. It was soft and comfy, and she wrapped it around herself like a sarong. While she was up, she gathered her clothing, and folded everything into a neat pile. Then she returned to the rug and watched the fire.

Duke came back wearing a pair of gray sweatpants and carrying an open bottle of wine, two glasses and a sack of potato chips.

"Hungry?" he asked with a smile as he joined her on the rug.

"I am totally, happily content in every sense of the word," she responded pertly. "But I suppose I could eat one or two potato chips."

"Or ten or twenty?" Duke was pouring wine into the glasses.

She laughed lightly. "Never can tell."

Duke handed her a glass and raised his own. "Here's to us."

"Umm...yes, okay. To us."

After a swallow of wine, Duke put down his glass and tore the potato chip bag open. "Help yourself."

"Thanks." Lola took a chip.

"It's raining harder," Duke said.

Lola glanced to a window. "Yes, it is." Her gaze returned to Duke. "Did you have any flooding from yesterday's downpour?"

He gave his head a shake. "Some. Nothing dangerous."

"That's good."

"Yes, it is. I remember one spring—I was about seventeen, I think—when all of our low fields had a foot of water. Lost a lot of hay that year. It doesn't happen very often, thank goodness."

"I think I remember the year you're talking about. Weren't some roads flooded out, too?"

"Sure were."

"School was dismissed for several days because the buses couldn't get to some of the rural areas." Lola smiled. "Us town kids were thrilled, I recall."

"How old are you, Lola?"

She put on a deliberately haughty expression. "A gentleman *never* asks a lady's age."

Duke popped a chip into his mouth. "I bet I'm ten years older than you are. I'm thirty-four."

"If you were seventeen when the area flooded and I can remember it, how could you be ten years older? I was nine when I came to Montana."

Duke thought a moment, calculating time and ages. "Okay, then you must be getting close to thirty. You don't look it."

"Thank you very much." Lola grinned impishly and took a sip of wine.

"You're not going to tell me your age, are you?"

"Nope."

"You're a tease, Lola Fanon."

"Sometimes," she said with a laugh. "Do you mind?"

He shook his head. "I love you just the way you are."

Lola's smile vanished. "Duke, maybe you're kidding and maybe you're not, but I'm not ready to talk about love."

"You'll make love with me but not *talk* about love?"

"I'm sure you've made love to women and not talked about love before," she said quietly.

"Yeah, but..." He stopped to gather his thoughts and ended up pinning her with a probing look. "But I don't think you have. You're not the type."

"Didn't you say several times that you and I are very much alike?"

"And didn't you say we weren't? Besides, I wasn't talking about every aspect of our lives."

"In other words, it's all right that you made love to a zillion women but it wouldn't be all right if I had slept with a lot of men."

"I never made love to a zillion women, Lola. Don't exaggerate."

The humor had gone out of their conversation. From his expression and voice, she could tell that he'd become deadly serious.

Fine. So would she be. "Let me tell you how it is, Duke. I like you or I wouldn't be here, but I won't be pressured or sweet-talked into anything. I don't want our relationship to end, so please don't misunderstand. But I want to give it plenty of time. *I* want time."

"How much time?"

"At this point I have no idea."

"What are your reservations?"

She blinked, startled by his question. "Umm...I'm not sure."

"Don't con me, Lola. You want time for some reason, and I can't believe you don't know what that reason is. Are you afraid of commitment? Afraid of me? Uneasy because things are happening so fast for us? Or maybe you just don't have the same kind of feelings for me that I have for you. Though, to tell you the truth, I never would have believed that a few minutes ago. Nor this morning or the first time we made love. We connect, baby. We connect the way every couple wishes they could. You know it, I know it.''

Lola's face got pink and flushed. "We connect in one area, Duke, sex. I'm not denying that. Obviously my reservations don't lie in that area of our relationship."

He was watching her broodingly. "You're saying we can go on as we are if I don't talk about the future."

"In regard to us," she added. "Talk about the future all you want. Talk about anything you want. Just don't expect more from me than I can give." Her eyes met his. "Is that really asking too much?"

He gave a short, sharp laugh. "It's asking a hell of a lot. I'm not just fooling around with you, Lola. You mean the world to—"

"Stop it," she said sharply.

His brooding stare continued through several silent seconds. Then he took a breath. "You're a peculiar woman."

She wasn't at all insulted. In fact, she was thinking that he was finally beginning to understand her. "I've always marched to a different drummer, Duke. If that's a problem for you, then I'm sorry, but it's your problem, not mine."

"In other words, you have no intention of adjusting any of your viewpoints to fit mine."

Lola thought a moment. "That's one way of putting it. I think a better way is for two people to accept each other exactly as they are. That adjustment business can lean much too far in one person's favor." Her expression became sober and serious. "Do you intend to change any attitudes or viewpoints for me?"

He frowned. "I don't have any peculiar attitudes."

She picked up her glass from where she'd placed it on the rug and took a swallow of wine. "You've just proven my point."

"And just what do you mean by that?"

"That you consider yourself perfect."

"Don't be absurd. No one's perfect."

"If not perfect, then without peculiarities," Lola amended.

"Okay, if you think I've got peculiarities, tell me what they are," he demanded.

She looked at him for a long time, then shook her head. "No, I think I'll let you figure them out for yourself."

His mind raced, wondering what he'd done that she considered peculiar. Dammit, he was as normal as they came. What in hell was she talking about?

Lola didn't miss his glower. "Now you're angry. Would you like me to leave?"

His eyes narrowed. "All you want from me is sex."

He had startled her, but she recovered quickly. "For the present, yes."

He shoved the potato chip sack aside, set down his glass and got to his feet. "In that case, what are we waiting for? Come on, babe, let's go to bed."

The tone of his voice wasn't at all flattering. She eluded the hand he held out and scrambled to her feet on her own.

"I think it's time for me to leave," she said coolly, moving to her stack of clothing. "I'll dress in the bathroom."

Before she could pick anything up, he hauled her into his arms. His eyes were dark and simmering. "You came here for sex. Why leave now, just when we've got everything figured out and in the open?"

She wriggled to get free, but he held her in place. "You haven't figured out anything. Let go of me, Duke. I don't like you like this."

"Meaning you've had enough sex for today? When will you want stud service again, babe, tomorrow, the next day? Should I wait for your call, or what?"

She gasped. "How dare you speak to me that way?"

"It's your doing, dammit!" He couldn't remember when he'd ever been so wounded over anything. He loved this maddening woman and she only wanted sex from him.

Afraid that he might do something he would most definitely regret later, he abruptly pushed her away.

"Go on. Get the hell out of here," he growled.

Lola picked up her clothes. "Why are you so angry?"

"Figure it out for yourself," he told her, his eyes snapping with all the fury and anguish he was feeling. Then he started for the doorway. "I'm sure you can find your own way out," he tossed back over his shoulder.

With her heart in her throat, Lola watched him leave the room. Then her own anger kicked in. "Jerk," she muttered as she picked up her bundle of clothing.

In five minutes she was outside and heading for her car. It wasn't until she was driving down Duke's driveway to the road that the tears began, surprising and angering her.

But no matter how often she wiped them away, there were more dribbling down her cheeks.

Now, why in God's name was she crying over a jerk? Again.

Eleven

———

Lola beat Charlie home. She wasn't worried about him, as the Burnhams were avid pinochle players and had no doubt gotten Charlie into a marathon card game. Actually, she was glad she didn't have to go in and pretend everything was peachy when it wasn't.

She stopped just inside the kitchen door as an unnerving thought struck her: this was the very first time that she couldn't bring a problem to Charlie with every honesty.

Her lips pursed as she continued on through the house to her bedroom. What had ever made her think Duke was broad-minded enough to handle an affair? What had made *her* think of an affair at all, when it had been perfectly obvious all along that he was leaning toward serious? Besides, her very own attitude had recently been far adrift of who she really was. Just when had she put sex into such a casual category?

Annoyed with herself as much as with Duke, she undressed, put on a robe and headed for the bathroom and a shower. Fifteen minutes later, feeling a little less stressed out, she returned to her bedroom to pull on a gray-and-green sweat suit. She was just slipping into a pair of canvas shoes when the telephone rang.

Her lips thinned again. It was Duke, she would bet on it. Calling to talk her into thinking that nothing had happened to make her upset or angry. She should just let the damned phone ring until he got tired of listening to it, she thought peevishly.

Then she sighed. There was no guarantee it was Duke; it could be any number of friends or even Serena again. Maybe Charlie.

Her expression was sullen when she picked up the phone. "Hello?"

"Lola?"

Lola frowned at the thin little voice in her ear. It was familiar but that was all.

"Yes, this is Lola."

The voice caught with a sob. "I . . . I'm sorry. I told myself I was going to be brave about this, but . . ."

Recognition hit Lola. "Candace?"

"Yes, it's me. Oh, Lola." Candace broke down into sobs.

Lola's forehead creased with an even deeper frown. Something was wrong. Her first thought was that Ron's work had finally caused a major rift between him and his wife, and Candace had called for solace.

But from the little she knew of Candace, or Candy, as Ron always called her, she wasn't the type of woman to call long distance from Germany to seek comfort from her husband's family over a marital disagreement.

Lola's heart began pounding with an awful premonition. "Candace, please tell me what's wrong," she said as gently as she could manage, given the sudden tide of panic rising in her throat.

"Yes . . . I must," Candace sobbed. "Is Charlie there?"

"No, just me."

"Oh. I wish he was there so I could tell you both at the same time. Lola . . . I . . . I've lost Ron. We all have."

Lola could hear her frantic heartbeat in her own ears. "Candace, are you saying...?" She couldn't finish the question.

"He's dead, Lola. Oh, God, I can't bear it." Candace began sobbing again.

Lola's system went into denial. Ron couldn't be dead. He was young and strong and healthy.

Her legs suddenly gave out and she sank weakly to the edge of the bed. *Charlie,* she thought. *Oh, Charlie.*

"Candace, please, you must tell me what happened," she said in a hoarse, tear-clogged voice.

"Yes...yes. Give me a minute."

Lola could tell that Candace had put down the phone. Waiting for her to pick it up again, Lola's mind battled with a dozen frenzied ideas and questions. How would she tell Charlie? Someone would have to call Serena. What about funeral arrangements? Was Candace emotionally capable of dealing with what had to be done? What *would* have to be done?

"Oh, God," she moaned. What worse tragedy could befall a family?

Candace came on the line again. Her voice was thick and unsteady, but she was speaking more coherently.

"I'm sorry. I was notified four hours ago by two officers that Ron was killed in the line of duty. They were sympathetic but quite formal, and they would not tell me what he'd been doing to put him in danger. They said his work was a matter of national security and international consequences. He was shot, Lola. They want to ship him— his...his body to Washington for burial at Arlington. I don't believe it's their decision to make. I need to talk to Charlie."

"I understand," Lola said in a near whisper. She was trying desperately to maintain self-control. "He's visiting friends, Candace. I'll call him immediately. I'm sure he'll call you back right away. Are you all right? And the baby?"

"Little Ron is fine. He's too young to...understand."

"Yes, of course. Candace, we love you and are here for you always. Never lose sight of that." Candace had no family of her own, so this was probably the only call she would make to the States. "I'm going to hang up now and call Charlie."

"All right. I'll be waiting to hear from him. Goodbye, Lola . . . and thank you."

"Goodbye for now, Candace." Lola put the phone down and then moaned and covered her face with her hands. Sobs shook her shoulders. How would the family survive this horrible blow? Ron, dear Ron. Memories of him, big, gruff and laughing, created unbearable pain.

But she couldn't sit here and feed her own grief; she had to call Charlie. Getting up for tissues to wipe her eyes and blow her nose, Lola returned to the phone. She had to look up the Burnhams' number in the phone book, and her hands were shaking so hard it was difficult to do.

She finally located the number and, drawing a deep breath, dialed it. A lilting female voice answered. "Hello?"

"Mrs. Burnham?"

"This is she. What can I do for you?"

"This is Lola Fanon. Is Charlie still there?"

"He certainly is. Beating the pants off of us at pinochle, I might add."

She *couldn't* tell him on the phone, she just couldn't. "Mrs. Burnham, would you please tell him that I must see him at once? Ask him to come home right away."

"Well, yes, dear, of course. Is something wrong?"

"Something is very wrong, Mrs. Burnham. Please send him home right away."

"I'll do it this very minute."

"Thank you. Goodbye." Lola put the phone down before Mrs. Burnham could ask any more questions. Then she sat there, stupefied. Serena had to be told, but Charlie first. She collapsed into sobs again. How could she tell Charlie that his only son was dead?

Candace had known for four hours before she called. She probably hadn't been able to talk about it with anyone when she first heard. Oh, poor Candace. And poor little Ron, growing up without his father.

But she must pull herself together before Charlie got home. Hurrying to the bathroom, Lola bathed her eyes with cool water. Then, looking at herself in the mirror, she thought of Duke, and that she would like to talk to him. He was so strong, and right now she needed his strength. She needed *him*.

"Oh, no," she whispered as she realized for the first time that she loved him. *Really* loved him. Why had she fought so hard against it? Why know the truth so clearly now, after she had probably destroyed their relationship? Had it taken a shock of this magnitude to jar her senses?

Depressed beyond belief, she went to the kitchen and put on a pot of coffee, anything to keep busy until Charlie got home.

Then she heard his car, and every cell in her body went rigid. In seconds Charlie was bounding through the door, an expression of concern on his face. "Lola, what's wrong?"

She licked her dry lips. "Come and sit down, Uncle Charlie. There's something I have to tell you."

On Monday morning Lola went to her store at the usual time. Betty walked in five minutes later with a cheery "Hi."

"Hi, Betty."

Betty's cheerful smile faded. "Uh-oh. Something's wrong. Is it the robbery?"

"No." After a heavy sigh, Lola told her the awful story. "I have to go home and help Charlie make some decisions. I really hate to ask after the robbery on Saturday, but can you handle the store by yourself this morning? Are you afraid to be here alone?"

"Absolutely not. If some other idiot decided to rob the store, Lola, he'd probably try it if there were ten people working in here." Betty looked on the verge of tears. "Oh, Lola, I feel so bad for you and your family. I knew Ron. Not well, but I remember when he played football on the high school team. I'm so very sorry."

"Thank you." Lola brushed away a tear. "Charlie was up half the night. I know he called Candace several times. He was finally sleeping this morning when I had to leave, so I really don't know what's going on. I'll come back here as soon as I can."

"Don't hurry on my account," Betty said.

Lola left the building and got in her car. But she didn't start it. Why had she even opened the store this morning? Habit? Routine? She really didn't want to worry about Betty being alone, or if sales were good or about any other aspect of the business.

Determinedly she got out and walked back into the store. "Betty, I've changed my mind. I'm going to close the store for a few days." Walking over to the front door, she locked it and put the Closed sign back in place. "I should have thought this through before coming in this morning. Before letting you come in."

"Lola, you don't have to explain anything to me. I understand what you're going through. Just call me when you're ready to reopen, okay?"

"I will, and thank you."

After Lola made some calls to notify her part-time help of the store's closure—mostly talking to parents as the teenagers were in school—she and Betty walked out the back entrance together. Lola drove home thinking of the awful night Charlie must have suffered. She herself hadn't slept well and had heard Charlie moving around the house or talking on the phone every time she awakened. But she had stayed in bed, as Charlie had seemed to want to be alone. Once the initial shock of the news she'd passed on to him had really sunk in, he had gone to his room. She had never seen him so gray and pasty, and she feared for his well-being.

She'd respected his apparent need for privacy last night. But now she wanted to be with him, needed to be with him. And there must be something she could do to help him get through this.

She walked into the house to see Charlie on the kitchen telephone. Pouring herself a cup of coffee, she stood by and listened to his end of a conversation with a travel agent.

He finally put down the phone and looked at her. "I'm going to Germany, Lola. Candace and I talked several times, and we've come to the conclusion that Ron should be buried here, in his hometown. It's what we both want. I'm going to bring Candace and the baby back with me to live here. I'm all packed and will be leaving at once. I called Serena, and she'll be flying in today or tomorrow, as soon as she can arrange her schedule. She'll let you know so you can meet her plane. The funeral is set for three days from now. Candace is handling the legalities and military regulations on her end. We should be home in two days.''

He got up and put his arms around Lola. ''Keep things going here, honey,'' he said huskily. ''I'd like you to fix up Ron's room to accommodate his family.''

Nearly choked by unshed tears, Lola hoarsely agreed. ''It will be ready, Charlie. I promise.''

He kissed her cheek. ''I love you, honey.''

''And I love you, Charlie.''

''Our family might be a little smaller, but we've got to stick together.''

''Yes, and we will,'' she whispered tearily, vowing it in her soul.

Duke kept calling the store and getting no answer. He couldn't figure it out. It was Monday and Lola's store should be open. Would she actually ignore the telephone to avoid talking to him, just in case he called? It seemed like an absurd idea, but there had to be some reason why she wasn't answering.

It honestly never occurred to him that the store might not be open until midafternoon. At first he ridiculed that idea. Lola Fanon not adhere to duty and routine? Never! Even if she got the flu or something, she had good help. No, if that store wasn't open, there was another reason than Lola not feeling well.

Charlie would know what was going on, Duke decided then. He headed for the house and the telephone again, having worried enough about it.

Only, there was no answer at Charlie's house, either. ''What the hell?'' Duke muttered, putting down the phone after six rings. If Lola's store was closed, and Charlie's Place was closed, something bad had to have happened within the Fanon family. Duke's heart turned over in his chest as speculation about what it could be made his skin crawl.

Hurrying to his bathroom, he threw off his work clothes and took a shower. Dressed in clean clothing, he tore through the house, stopping only long enough to tell June he was going to town.

Then he was on his way, driving faster than normal, his lips set in a thin, grim line. If something had happened to Lola, he didn't think he'd be able to bear it, but would try for Charlie's sake. And if Charlie was ill or something, he should be at Lola's side.

Whatever was going on, he was going to be a part of it, that much was certain.

After Charlie left for the airport in Billings, Lola changed into jeans and an old T-shirt, went to Ron's room, stepped inside and then, seeing all of his high school and college mementos on the walls and shelves, collapsed on his bed to cry her heart out.

Eventually she was calmer and able to sit up and think with some clarity. Charlie wanted her to make this room comfortable for Candace and the baby. It was her own decision to pack away the many reminders that would only make Candace feel worse than she already did.

Locating some clean, sturdy cardboard boxes in Charlie's storage room, Lola took everything off the walls and shelves of Ron's room. She taped the boxes shut as they were filled, and was in and out of the house for several hours, carrying them to the garage to stack them in a corner. Candace would want Ron's things, and someday she would feel strong enough to go through these boxes.

Some of Ron's old clothes still hung in the closet, and Lola packed them in a box, as well. She was just returning to the house from the garage when she heard the phone ringing. Running to pick it up, it stopped ringing just as she reached it.

"Oh, damn," she muttered, worried that the caller was Serena with her flight information. Charlie should have an answering machine, darn it. Everyone had an answering machine these days. Other people might have called while she was in the garage, as well, but missing Serena's call was unforgivable. Fretting about it for a few minutes, she then sat at the kitchen extension and placed a call to Serena's Washington number. When there was no answer she put down the phone with a frown. It could have been Serena calling from someplace other than her apartment, but Lola had no idea where that someplace might be.

Sighing, she got up and returned to Ron's room. She put fresh bedding on the bed, dusted the furniture and vacuumed the carpet. Observing the result of her efforts, she decided the room looked too bare now. From various places in the house, she brought in pretty knickknacks to set on the shelves, and some framed pictures to hang on the walls.

And then it occurred to her that there was no place for the baby to sleep. She called Betty.

"Betty, I remember your saying one time that you still have the crib your children used as infants. Would you mind if I borrowed it for a short time? I'm sure Candace's own things will be shipped to Rocky Ford, but in the meantime..."

Betty cut in. "Of course you can borrow the crib. And I also have a high chair and other things the kids used as babies. I'll have Tom bring them by when he gets home from work. Should be around six, six-thirty."

"Thanks, Betty. You're a lifesaver."

"Call me if there's anything else Tom or I can do, Lola. Anything at all."

"I will, Betty, thank you."

It was good to have friends at a time like this, Lola thought sadly while putting down the phone. It startled her by ringing before she had even let go of it.

Quickly she brought it to her ear. "Hello?"

"This is Serena, Lola. How are you holding up?" Serena's sad voice said.

"Probably the same as you. Oh, Serena, this is so terrible."

They wept for a moment, then cleared their throats and wiped their eyes. "I have my flight schedule, Lola," Serena said unsteadily.

"I have a pad and pencil right here. Give it to me." Lola scribbled down the information Serena recited.

"Dad already left for Germany?" Serena asked.

"Hours ago."

"Lola . . . how is he, really?"

"He's . . . bearing up, Serena. That's really all I can say. There's so much to do and he's going to see that it's done."

"He's always been so strong," Serena said on a sob. "But this . . ."

"I know," Lola said. "We're going to have to be strong for him, Serena. And for Candace. Think of what she must be going through. Before Charlie left, he hugged me and said something about the family sticking together. That's very important to him."

"It's important to all of us, Lola. Well . . . I have a hundred things to do before I get on that plane. See you tomorrow, all right?"

"I'll be at the airport. Bye, Serena."

"Bye, Lola."

Lola hung up, put her head back and closed her teary eyes. But thinking of the ordeal they all faced was so unnerving, she couldn't sit still for long. Rising, she hurried down the hall to take a shower.

Duke pulled his four-wheeler into the Fanon driveway; Charlie's pickup was absent and Lola's car was parked in its usual spot. He had driven by the store and seen the Closed sign, then come directly to the Fanon home.

He got out slowly, almost cautiously, painfully concerned about something, though what it could be was pure conjecture. But it was obvious that Charlie's Place wasn't open, either, and those two Closed signs boded no good.

Walking around to the back of the house, he climbed the porch stairs and rapped on the door. Admittedly his heart was in his throat. He'd never felt so wired before, not even when his father had fallen ill and his nerves had jumped around like butter on a hot skillet.

But this was different. This involved Lola, whatever "this" was, and he actually tasted the acrid flavor of fear in his mouth.

His eyes widened when the door opened and there she was, looking perfectly healthy in a green-and-white checked cotton robe.

"Lola," he said in a voice that was as weak with relief as his knees.

From his ashen color and peculiar voice, she could only surmise that he'd come here with bad news. And she didn't have the strength for any more bad news.

Before she could say so, however, he asked, "Do you know where Charlie is?"

The anxiety she heard behind his question was alarming. "Why?" she said sharply. Oh, God, if something had happened to Charlie, such as an accident on his way to the airport, she would crumple and never recover.

"Why?" Duke echoed numbly. "Because his place is closed. Because *your* store is closed. Lola, what in hell is going on? Is Charlie all right?"

Wearily she brushed her damp hair back from her forehead. He wasn't here with bad news; he was here to *hear* bad news. "Come in," she said, stepping back so he could enter the house.

Duke came in, took two steps and stopped while Lola closed the door. She turned to look at him, and it was then that he noticed the signs of sorrow in her eyes.

"Ron's dead," she said without preamble.

"Ron? Your cousin? Charlie's son?"

"Yes," she said dully. "Charlie's on his way to Germany to . . . to . . ." She couldn't go on. "Oh, Duke," she whispered. "He's dead."

"My God," Duke mumbled, and rushed forward to take her into his arms. Holding her, he felt her shoulders shaking with silent sobs. Tenderly he caressed her hair, her back. "Lola, I'm so sorry," he whispered emotionally.

She said nothing, just clung to him as though he were some sort of lifeline and wept into his shirt. He wanted some answers—how Ron died, for one—but he couldn't bring himself to ask. When Lola calmed, she would talk about it; he could wait to learn the facts of the awful tragedy.

So he just stood there and let her take what comfort she could from him. It was encouraging that she had turned to him for comfort, and he wanted to say that he would always be available through any curve life might throw at her.

Finally her weeping stopped, but she didn't move away from him. Instead, she snuggled closer and whispered raggedly, "I need you. I need you so much right now."

For the merest second his spine stiffened. Hadn't he told her only yesterday not to come to him if stud service was all she wanted from him?

But he loved her too much to be cruel, especially today. Besides, he wanted her, too. He would *always* want her, no matter how many insults they threw at each other.

"Will you?" she whispered.

"You know I will," he said, more harshly than he'd intended. "Which way to your bedroom?"

She took his hand. "I'll show you."

He went but he wasn't sure how to take Lola's mood. It seemed sensible to assume that because of overwhelming grief, her real need was closeness with another human being. But would just any man do? Maybe he was merely a handy outlet for her emotional tension. Long ago he'd read something about the loss of a loved one making a person seek reassurance of his or her own life. Everyone did it in different ways, of course. Apparently Lola's way was to take him to her bedroom.

He stood by while she closed the window blinds. Then, teary-eyed, she opened her robe and let it fall to the floor. He sucked in a sharp breath. Her beauty astounded him, as it had the first time he'd seen her, as it would until the day of his own passing.

It suddenly didn't matter why she was doing this. Hastily he began undressing. She pulled back the bed covers and lay

down, never taking her eyes off him. He stared at her just
as intently while frenetically tearing off his clothes.

And then she did something so erotic, so sexually incit-
ing, he thought his heart would burst through his rib cage.
She slowly brought her knees up and then let them fall
apart, and he found himself looking directly at her most
private spot.

"Lola..." He said her name in a hoarse croak that he
barely recognized as his own voice. Finally down to his un-
dershorts, he got rid of them and all but leaped onto the
bed, lowering his hard and throbbing erection precisely into
the arousing view she had just given him.

Their passion exploded into mindless action. Kissing her
with all the hunger of a man who had never kissed a woman
before, he thrust into her and began moving. Her finger-
nails scored his back. He bit her lips and sucked on her
breasts. It was rough and hot, and neither held anything
back. Words were whispered between them that neither used
in public.

Lola twisted and writhed beneath him, panting and
gasping, moaning and whimpering. Nothing was enough.
She wanted all of him. She wanted to feel completely possessed, completely overpowered. Taking two handfuls of his
hair, she yanked his head down for a kiss and plunged her
tongue deeply into his mouth.

Duke was no stranger to passion, but never had he been
with a wilder woman. It increased his own wildness, and he
finally took her hands, held them over her head and rode her
so hard the bed groaned in protest, the headboard bump-
ing the wall with a pounding beat.

"Is this what you want?" he growled thickly.

"Yes...yes," she gasped. "Make me a part of you."

He did his best to comply, and when she finally cried out,
she also began crying. His climax was right behind hers, and
he fell forward, catching her in his arms to let her cry on his
shoulder.

Her sobs slowly subsided until she was merely sniffling.
Then he heard, "I need a tissue."

He raised his head. Her eyes were red, wet and puffy, but she still looked beautiful to him. "I'll get you some tissues, if you'll tell me where they are," he said gently.

"Thanks, but I need to get up. We didn't use protection again."

Groaning, he rolled to the bed.

Twelve

———

Lola was waiting at the gate when Serena deplaned in Billings. Neither smiled at the other, but they walked into each other's arms and hugged for a long emotional moment. There were no tears. Lola had cried herself out and Serena looked as though she'd done the same.

They walked to the baggage department and waited for Serena's suitcases. "Have you heard anything from Dad?" she asked her cousin.

"No, but I'm really not expecting to. He brought his pickup here to the airport, and I would imagine he and Candace are very busy. From what he said before he left, they should be coming in tomorrow. Exhausted, probably."

"Yes, exhausted," Serena murmured. "I know I am and you look tired, too." She heaved a long sigh. "It's impossible to sleep with so much on your mind. Oh, there's one of my cases."

When the other suitcase appeared, they carried the luggage out to Lola's car and stowed it in the trunk. Then they got in the front seat and Lola started the drive to Rocky Ford. For a while they were both silent, with Serena staring out the side window and Lola watching the road.

She was also thinking of something. After their frantic lovemaking yesterday, Duke had said, "What if you got pregnant during one of our times together?" She had answered, "I can't think about that now."

She didn't want to think about it today, either, but it kept popping into her mind. They had been careless about using protection twice; pregnancy was a definite possibility.

She sighed, drawing Serena's attention. Before Serena could ask what had brought on that heavy sigh, though, she asked Serena, "How's your friend, Edward?"

Serena frowned a little. "Well...I'm not sure I know how to answer that. Oh, he's well. I don't mean to imply anything wrong with him health-wise, but..." She, too, heaved a sigh. "I don't know, Lola. I love him madly, but he's so peculiar about some things."

"Aren't we all?" God knew she had her peculiar moments, and Duke? Well, Duke might not be correctly diagnosed as peculiar, but he wasn't your common, everyday Joe, either.

"To a degree, yes. But Edward..." Serena stopped. "Oh, never mind. I'm probably just being petty, and who's interested, anyway?" She turned to look at Lola. "Tell me how Rocky Ford's been holding up during my absence."

So that was how they passed the drive home, in idle chatter. They knew they couldn't talk about Ron without bawling, and each felt cried out. Their personal lives also held some problems, and neither was of a frame of mind to talk about problems of any kind. Not when they were saturated with what they were going to have to deal with in the next couple of days.

Serena did smile once, when Lola drove into Charlie's driveway. "Home," Serena murmured. "It's always here, isn't it?"

"I felt the same when I returned," Lola told her. She reached out and squeezed her cousin's hand. "Let's go in and get you settled."

After dinner and baths, Serena and Lola sat in the living room in their nightclothes. Lola had produced a bottle of wine, and they were sipping from tulip glasses. The house was quiet, as neither wanted the TV or radio on. They spoke in muted tones. Lola had just told Serena about the robbery.

Serena shuddered. "You must have been terrified."

"Actually...no. I was frightened at first, but then I wasn't. I can't explain it. Maybe when it comes down to survival, a person's courage emerges."

"Not in every case. I would say you're one of those fortunate people who can think clearly in a crisis."

"Well, you are too, Serena."

"Am I? I don't know, Lola. I think that's something you know only after the fact. Anyway, I'm really proud of how you handled the situation."

Lola was studying her cousin, who had glorious red hair with a soft natural curl and a creamy, flawless complexion. "Do you know that you look prettier every time I see you?"

Serena shaped a small smile. "Thanks, cuz, but I can say the same about you. I love your short hairstyle. I've been thinking about having some of my mop cut off. What do you think? Should I or shouldn't I?"

"You shouldn't," Lola replied emphatically. "Your hair is special, Serena."

They chatted about this and that through two glasses of wine. Feeling relaxed for the first time in days, Lola brought her legs up under her on the sofa. She'd been thinking of Duke off and on, but hadn't mentioned him.

Serena did that by saying, "Who's this man you said something about on the phone?"

"Did I say something about a man?"

"When I told you about Edward, you said—"

"Oh, yes, now I remember." Lola looked down at her glass of wine. "I don't know what to say about him, Serena, except..." Her gaze lifted. "I think I'm in love with him and I'm not sure I want to be."

"Why not? Is there something wrong with him? Who is he?"

"Duke Sheridan. Do you remember the name?"

"The Sheridan Ranch?"

"Right. And I guess there's nothing really wrong with him. I mean, he's very handsome and sexy, but..."

"But what?" Serena prompted.

Lola heaved a sigh. "He...he's just so darned opinionated."

"And you're not, of course."

In spite of the weight of grief in her heart, Lola had to laugh. "That sounds funny, but it's really the crux of my problem. We're *both* opinionated, and those opinions seldom coincide." Her expression sobered. "Serena, I could never marry a man who wholeheartedly believed in his right to order me around." She pinned her cousin with a challenging look. "Could you?"

"I'd like to think not. But what does a woman do if she falls in love?"

"Are you thinking of Edward now?" Lola asked.

Serena sighed. "I guess so."

"Does he order you around?"

"Subtly, tactfully, but yes. It's his work. There's so much of his life I can't be a part of. It's very frustrating."

"Well, Duke is not tactful," Lola said grimly.

Serena smiled impishly. "But is he a good lover?"

For a second they were teenagers again, exchanging secrets and giggling over them. "That's what I asked you on the phone about Edward, isn't it? Yes, he's a good lover. He's an incredible lover."

Lola's answer struck a serious note, and their moment of levity passed, with each woman thinking her own thoughts.

Lola got to her feet. "It's late. We should go to bed."

Serena agreed. They brought the empty wine bottle and their glasses to the kitchen, then said good-night and went to their bedrooms.

It was a long time before Lola fell asleep.

The woman in room 116 of the Sundowner Motel laid the newspaper out on the little round table near the window and sipped from a can of soda while she read.

*An article on the third page stopped her cold. Her heart
raced wildly as she read.*

Local Man Killed In Germany

Ronald John Fanon, son of Charles Fanon, died from
a gunshot wound in Frankfurt, Germany. Ronald made
a career with the military, and his death was in the line
of duty, though the Army is not releasing any details
concerning the tragic event. Ronald leaves a wife,
Candace; a son, Ronald, Jr.; his father, Charles; a sister, Serena; and a cousin, Lola. Many people in Rocky
Ford will remember Ron Fanon with great affection.
Services will take place at the Christian Church on Fifth
Street on Thursday at 1:00 p.m. Friends are welcome to
attend.

*The woman sat there stunned. So much family. She'd had
no idea. And Ron, a person she hadn't even known existed,
was dead.*

*Rising finally, she went to the window, leaned against the
frame and stared out, sadly pondering all that she was
learning about the Fanon family.*

*She made a decision: she would attend that funeral. All
the Fanons would be in one place, under one roof. The
church would be full. No one would notice her.*

*Yes, she thought, licking her dry, almost feverish lips. She
would definitely attend that funeral.*

Because of the obituary in the newspaper, the phone never
stopped ringing on Wednesday. Lola and Serena took turns
answering it, explaining again and again to Charlie's many
friends that he had gone to Germany to escort Ron's wife
and son back to Montana. Yes, he would be back today, and
no, they didn't know his exact arrival time.

They were also doing some housecleaning and answering
the door. The amount of food delivered by friends was
astonishing: cakes, pies, salads, casseroles, a whole ham, a
smoked turkey—the list was endless and the refrigerator and
pantry were bulging.

"Everyone will come here after the service," Lola told her cousin. Eyeing yet another huge sheet cake just delivered, she added, "At least I hope they will. We have enough food to feed the whole town."

Charlie, Candace and little Ron arrived around four. There were hugs and tears among the women, and a hug for Lola and Serena from Charlie. Ronnie, who was fourteen months old, slid out of his mother's arms to the floor and began to explore. Candace started after him.

"Let him be," Charlie told her with a loving look at his grandson. "What can he hurt? And it's only natural for him to be curious about his new home."

Candace, petite, blond and beautiful, looked utterly done in. Lola took charge. "Candace, you should lie down. Serena and I will watch Ronnie. Charlie, you should rest, too."

Neither of them put up an argument; the long trip had been exhausting. They showed Candace to her and the baby's room, and she thanked Lola for the crib. In the kitchen was a high chair and a playpen, and she thanked Lola for those items, as well.

Then they left her alone. Charlie went to his room. Ronnie didn't seem at all tired, and Lola and Serena fondly followed the little boy around while he examined everything he came across.

"He's adorable," Serena said quietly. "He has Ron's eyes and mouth."

"And his mother's hair," Lola added. Indeed he was an adorable child. Tears suddenly filled her eyes, and she turned away.

Serena saw, however, and she put her arms around her cousin. "I know what you're feeling," she said softly.

They both knew. This beautiful little boy would have to grow up without his father.

It was reason enough for tears.

The funeral had the quiet chaos of most funerals. Emotion ran high and sobs could be heard throughout the flower bedecked church. After that came the graveside service, with too many people in attendance to pick out any one person.

It passed in a blur for Lola, and she could tell it was the same for the rest of the Fanon family. Candace clung to Charlie's arm throughout. Little Ron was absent, as Betty, bless her, had offered to stay at the house and watch the child.

Masses of people drove to Charlie's home when it was over. They crowded in to pay their respects to Ron's widow, and to ooh and aah over his sweet little son. The boy wasn't at all afraid of strangers, and was often the center of attention with his childish chortles and baby talk.

Surrounded by people, Lola happened to glance across the room. Duke, splendidly dressed in a dark suit, was shaking Charlie's hand. Then he moved to Candace and took her hand. Words were exchanged. Lola saw a wan smile appear on Candace's pretty face. Next he met Serena, and Lola all but held her breath. Serena was so beautiful. How could Duke not notice?

But then she saw him turn and search the crowd, finally spotting her. She nodded at him, and he began wending his way through the throng toward her.

Excusing herself, she headed for the bedroom wing, the only private area in the large house, knowing Duke would follow.

At the end of the hall, she stopped and leaned against a closet door, putting her head back and closing her eyes for a moment of much needed solitude. She felt weighted down by the day and the well-meaning horde of people.

Hearing footsteps on the carpet, she opened her eyes. "Hello."

"Hello," Duke said quietly. "How are you doing?"

"As well as can be expected."

"It was a nice service, Lola."

"Was it?" She could only remember bits and pieces of it. Maybe later, when everything was over with, she would remember it all, she thought. But for now, she didn't want to bring it into focus.

Duke hated the lost, forlorn look in her eyes. Her face was pale, appearing even paler because of the black dress she was wearing.

"I wish there was something I could do or say to make you feel better," he said, his gaze locked with hers.

"That's what everyone here wishes for the Fanon family, isn't it?" She sighed. "It will take time, Duke. Everyone's been through the loss of a loved one, everyone survives it. We'll survive it, too."

He swallowed nervously and kept staring at her. Her normal sparkle was notably missing. Her voice was dull and without its usual animation. Even her near-hysteria the day before yesterday, when she had hauled him to her bedroom, had been better than this lifeless mood of hers today.

He cleared his throat, thinking that there was one thing he could say that might snap her out of her misery. He took a step closer to her. They were standing no more than two inches apart.

"Lola," he whispered, "I love you."

She stared blankly.

"Did you hear what I said? I'm in love with you."

"I... love you, too." Her voice quavered.

He was stunned that it had been so easy. "You really do?" He wanted to take her in his arms, but a quick glance over his shoulder forestalled that idea. At the opposite end of the hall there were people, lots of people.

But no one was in the bedrooms, he remembered. Taking her hand, he led her to her room, quickly stepped inside and closed the door.

Then he put his arms around her. Inhaling deeply, she snuggled against him. His pulse quickened at once. "I love you," he said, repeating it in the next breath. "I love you." It felt so good to finally say it, and it seemed nothing short of a miracle that she loved him, too. "Tell me again that you love me," he whispered. "I need to hear it."

Had she said really that? she thought with a frown. Her mind was so dazed on this day of organized confusion. She couldn't doubt that he had said it, several times, but what had she said? Maybe he had misunderstood some incoherent remark she'd made.

Or maybe the truth of her feelings for him really had come out.

Her pulse was suddenly racing. Being in his arms was arousing, even on a day like this. He would forever affect her sexually. Maybe he *was* the man for her. The only man.

"I love you," she whispered.

"Oh, Lola, my love," he said hoarsely, tipping her chin for a kiss. His lips caressed hers with tenderness and a brand-new excitement. As she kissed him back with a passionate response, his blood rushed to his groin. Groaning, he kissed her again, harder, with more desire. Dare he go further? he wondered in the back of his mind. They were alone, and he wanted her desperately. There were so many people crammed into the house, who would miss either one of them?

But this was not the time or place for intimacy, so he just held her.

Her own desire gadually quieted, and finally she backed away. "There's so much to do. I shouldn't be in here with you."

"Lola, don't feel that way. We love each other."

Her nerves felt shattered. She darted to the mirror to check her hair and put on some lipstick. Her eyes met Duke's in the mirror. "Leave...please leave. We can't walk out of here together."

"Why not? We did nothing wrong. Don't be so worried." He made no move to leave. Instead he came up behind her and looked at her reflection in the mirror. "I'm asking you to marry me."

Her eyes got huge. "Today? Don't even think about it. Not today."

"All right, fine. I'll wait until tomorrow. What time should I come by?"

She moaned. "Duke, please. I can't even think straight. How do I know what tomorrow will bring to my family?"

He took her arm and turned her to look at him. "Lola, I'm coming by sometime tomorrow. And I'll propose right in front of your family, if I must."

"You wouldn't dare!"

"Try me."

By the look in his eyes, she knew he would do exactly that. She took a nervous breath. "All right. Come by after dinner tomorrow night. Around eight."

He nodded. "Great. I'll see you then." Dipping his head, he planted a kiss on her forehead. "I would have kissed your lips if you hadn't just put on lipstick. See you tomorrow night."

She stared numbly as he walked to the door, unlocked it and left.

Ten minutes later she was sitting on the bed, still dazed, when the door opened and Serena walked in.

"Oh, here you are." She hesitated. "Are you all right? This should be over soon, Lola. People are starting to leave."

"I...I had to get away by myself for a few minutes," Lola said, which wasn't a total lie.

"I understand completely. I don't know how Candace is holding up so well. She's apparently a lot stronger than she looks."

"She's a wonderful woman, Serena. I can see why Ron fell in love with her." Lola stood up. "I feel much better now. Let's return to the masses."

Arm in arm they left Lola's bedroom and walked down the hall to the gathering. Lola immediately searched the crowd for Duke, but he was nowhere in sight.

Breathing a relieved sigh because he had obviously gone, she went to the kitchen counter to help some people with servings of cake and coffee.

With her heart pounding madly, she slipped into the crowded house and then let herself be backed into a corner of the kitchen. From there she could see the entire Fanon family, other than the child. Her gaze went from Serena to Candace to Lola and then lingered on Charlie.

She studied his face, his gestures, and tried to read his lips above the din of so many voices as he spoke to various people. Even in grief his eyes and facial expressions were kindly. He laughed once when a man said something to him. She wished she had heard the remark, for in laughter Charlie's face came alive.

Someone spoke to her, a woman with a friendly smile. "I don't believe we've met."

"Uh, no," she said tersely. "But I must leave now. I'm sorry."

Quickly she squeezed through the throng and escaped through the kitchen door. Outside she hurried around the house and down the sidewalk to where she had parked her car. Only when she was seated behind the wheel did she breathe freely, and she marveled at her own audacity, her courage, in actually entering Charlie's home.

Yet, even with her courage expanding, the time wasn't right. It would come, she told herself, inserting the key in the ignition and starting the engine. It would come.

The morning was low-key and slowly paced. Everyone was tired and voices were quiet, actions unhurried. Candace was very attentive and loving to her son, which Lola admired. Serena was preparing to return to Washington and Charlie was going to drive her to the airport. Since there was so much leftover food, no one had to cook.

The afternoon was equally as quiet. After emotional goodbyes and promises to write, Serena left with Charlie to catch her plane in Billings, Candace took her son to their bedroom for a nap and Lola found herself completely alone. After tidying the kitchen, she decided on a walk. It was a bright, sunny day, and she figured she could do her worrying about Duke and tonight in the sunshine as well as in the house.

She returned two hours later, no closer to an answer for Duke than when she'd left. He was going to propose tonight, and what was she going to say?

Thirteen

Lola announced after dinner while they were still at the table that Duke would be picking her up at eight. Her eyes went to her uncle. "He... he's going to propose, Charlie."

Candace looked slightly startled but said nothing, merely spooned another bite of banana pudding into her son's waiting mouth.

Charlie cleared his throat. "Well, now," he said, scratching the back of his ear. "What would you like me to say, honey?"

Lola looked down at her plate. "I guess I just wanted you... to know."

"No, I think you want some advice. But I don't want to say the wrong thing, Lola. Do you love Duke?"

Lola swallowed. "I... yes."

"And he loves you?"

"He says he does."

"But you have reservations. Tell me about them if you wish, but I'm not going to ask what they are, Lola."

Lola smiled tremulously. "You're not going to tell me to accept or refuse."

"Only you can make that decision, honey," Charlie said gently.

Lola sighed. "I know." She smiled across the table at Candace. "Did you ever have any doubts about Ron?" Candace blanched and Lola stumbled over her own tongue to apologize. "Oh, Candace, forgive me. I don't know where my mind is these days."

"It's all right, Lola," Candace said with a reassuring little half smile. "I loved Ron and never had even one small doubt. I guess I was lucky." She paused. "In that regard, at least. But please promise me one thing, both of you." Her gaze went from Lola to Charlie and back. "I don't want either of you to avoid mentioning Ron because you're afraid hearing his name might hurt me. I want to remember him. I want never to forget him."

Lola nodded, although she felt about two inches high. Where *was* her mind these days? Look at how wishy-washy she was over Duke's impending proposal. She would bet that there were dozens of women in the area who would jump at the chance to go out with Duke Sheridan, let alone marry him.

But blurting out Ron's name to Candace so soon after his funeral was unbelievably thoughtless. She simply hadn't thought of him as gone when she'd asked that question. She wasn't herself anymore, and it was Duke's fault. Yes, she loved him and yes, she couldn't say no to him as far as sex went.

But marriage? She drew in a long breath. Marriage was forever, in her book. Was a constant itch for a man's body *really* love?

They were in Duke's four-wheeler, driving away from the house. "Any particular place you'd like to go?" Duke asked.

"No," Lola answered. "Just somewhere to talk...I suppose." Her heart was beating like a tom-tom. This was not going to be a casual conversation, and her trying to make it sound trivial was silly.

"We could go to the ranch."

She rolled her eyes. "Yes, and we both know what would happen if we were there alone for five minutes."

Duke chuckled deep in his throat. "You got that right, babe. Isn't it great?"

"Yes, great," she drawled dryly.

He sent her a glance. "Lola, I know you love me, so why not relax and enjoy it?"

He was right. She *did* love him, so she might as well stop throwing him those curves. She sighed. "I'm sorry."

"I know where to go," Duke said, and made a left turn onto a street that Lola knew led to the river.

He found a cozy little spot in the midst of a copse of trees, very close to the riverbank. Parking just so, he turned off the engine. The night quiet and the burbling of the slowly moving river water immediately permeated the interior of the vehicle.

Duke turned in the seat, laid his arm along the top of it and began toying with Lola's hair. "Pretty lady," he murmured.

She closed her eyes. His touch never failed to affect her, and though his hand was a long way from the pit of her stomach, that was where she felt it.

He slid over next to her and brought her head to his shoulder. His lips played over her face. "Say it," he whispered.

"Say what?"

"Lola, please don't play games. I love you and you told me you love me, too. Why are you avoiding saying it again?"

She sat there, silent and stony, for a few moments. Then she took a big breath. "All right, I love you. But—"

He hauled her close. "No buts, honey. That's all it takes to make a marriage. I love you so much I can't see straight. Will you marry me? The sooner the better, as far as I'm concerned."

"Duke, don't make it sound like some sort of race," she moaned, and covered her face with her hands.

"Hey, what's this?" Gently he pried her hands away from her face and held them. "Lola, you have to tell me exactly what you're feeling. I want to get married right away, but if you'd rather wait a few weeks..."

"A few weeks! I haven't even said yes yet."

A frown appeared between his eyes. "But you're going to, aren't you?"

She felt like bawling. Almost all of her wanted to say an unequivocal yes, but there was that one small part that kept resisting.

"Duke, we have to talk about... well, about things. Tell me your idea of marriage."

He sat back a little, puzzled over her request. "Marriage is marriage. What do you want me to say?"

"Isn't there anything you *want* to say?" She took an exasperated breath. "All right, tell me this. When you think of you and I married, what picture comes to your mind?"

He grinned. "That's easy. There are lots of pictures—the two of us eating together, riding horses together, talking, laughing, making love. Making love a lot," he repeated with a sexy little chuckle.

"And living where?" Lola prompted.

"At the ranch." He was suddenly worried. "I hope that's not a problem. Sweetheart, you'll love living at the ranch. I know you will."

"No, living at the ranch wouldn't be a problem. It's not that far from town," she said.

"Heck, it's only a short trip," Duke agreed. "Your family can come out and see you anytime they want, and you can run back and forth every day if—"

She broke in. "Well, of course I would be running back and forth every day. I could hardly operate the store from—"

"Operate the store!" he exclaimed with an indulgent laugh. "Honey, you'll be selling the store. I'll help you. You've got it in such great shape, I'm sure it'll sell real fast."

She felt as though an icy fist had started clutching her spine, and her voice reflected the chill in her backbone. "What makes you think I would sell the store? Duke, I wouldn't even *consider* selling my store!"

He looked shell-shocked. "But you'd have to. I want you with me, not in that damned store all day seven days a week."

"Six," she snapped. "You never have liked my being in business, have you?"

"I thought it was sort of...cute," he said lamely. "At first."

"Cute? *Cute?* Son of a—" She stopped herself from spouting the lineup of expletives in her mind. "Listen, do you have any idea what that store means to me? I'm making money. I could live out the rest of life on the money that store makes every week. And I could expand the operation. I could expand into women's wear...and into children's! I could open another store in Billings. In Missoula. In any damned town in any damned state. I could even franchise!"

Duke was weak. "Is...is that what you want to do?"

"Damned right it is! All along I knew you were a male chauvinist. What I didn't know was just how advanced the disease was!" Opening her door, she jumped out. "I'll find my own way home, thank you very much. And don't ever talk to me about love again. You've got some nerve. Your idea of love is...is hogwash!" She marched off into the dark.

Duke was too stunned to move. He sat there staring after her until he couldn't see her anymore. "Holy cow," he muttered, finally coming to. Sliding over to the wheel, he flashed on the headlights and started the engine. Lola was on the road, he knew that much, and he could only hope she wouldn't duck into the underbrush when she saw his car.

But she couldn't walk all the way home in the dark. Good Lord, it was almost ten miles. His lips set grimly as he amended his thoughts. If she decided to walk, then she'd walk. "Stubborn damn woman," he mumbled, recalling that he'd thought and said those words more than once where Lola was concerned.

Lola was doubting her own sanity. It was black as pitch on this country road, and she could barely see where to step. Relief rippled through her when she heard Duke's vehicle behind her, but with his headlights she could see just fine so she kept on walking.

He rolled down his window and drove alongside of her. "Get in, Lola. This is ridiculous."

"*You're* what's ridiculous," she retorted.

"Maybe I am, but your walking home isn't going to suddenly turn this frog into a prince. Get your butt into this car or so help me, I'll drag you in."

"You'd probably really do it, wouldn't you?" she fumed.

"Believe it."

"Fine. I'll get in. But don't you dare touch me."

"Lady, I wouldn't touch you with a ten-foot pole." He put on the brakes.

Lola marched around the front of the four-wheeler and got in. Duke took off so fast, the tires spun and kicked up gravel. She pretended not to notice and stared straight ahead.

But she couldn't remain silent. "You know, things bothered me about you all along—your possessive little remarks, your superior attitude. You don't think women have a brain at all, do you?"

"Don't be absurd," he said coldly.

"Well, you act like you don't."

"Because I think wives shouldn't work? Listen, babe, I happen to believe that a man should support his wife, and I won't apologize for it, either."

"That's the most archaic attitude I've ever heard of. I wouldn't be so proud of it, if I were you."

"No? What kind of man *would* you be proud of, Lola? A wimp who obeys your every command?"

"You're straying from the subject, in case you haven't noticed. And I'm not bossy, damn you, you are! Besides, we've already had that exact conversation." She fumed silently for a moment. "Since you're so opposed to working wives, I suppose you think *mothers* who dare to hold down jobs should be beheaded!''

"God save me from irrational women," Duke groaned.

For some reason the word *irrational* stopped Lola's tirade. Why, she was the most rational thinker she knew. She had *always* been a rational person.

Hadn't she?

Her silence went on for so long, Duke wondered if she was all right. He turned his head to peer at her in the dash lights, and she seemed okay. But why had she suddenly stopped shrieking at him?

"Look," he said in as even a tone as he could manage. "It never occurred to me that you wouldn't welcome a normal..." Stopping, he cleared his throat. "Forget that. What I'm trying to say is that I thought... No, forget that, too. Obviously I didn't think at all."

"Obviously," Lola agreed, though in a sane and sensible voice.

They had reached the outskirts of town. Taking heart from her calmer demeanor, Duke pulled the four-wheeler to the side of the road. Leaving the engine idling, he turned in the seat.

"Do we have a chance now?" he asked quietly.

Lola swallowed. "I... don't know."

"All right, let's put it another way. Do you *want* us to have a chance?"

"Do you?"

He kept looking at her, finally speaking. "More than anything."

She drew a deep breath. "Duke, I cannot and will not be dictated to. I could never live with a man who makes decisions all by himself about things that are near and dear to my heart."

"In other words, no man is ever going to take care of you."

"If what I just said sounds like that to you, then yes, you're right, no man is ever going to take care of me."

"That attitude could lead to a lot of cold and lonely nights," Duke said.

"So could yours." After a moment she reneged on that comment. "I take that back. I'm sure there are scores of women in this world who are praying for some man to come along and pamper them. That's not for me, Duke."

"And I'm just as positive that there are scores of men out there who would love to meet a woman who insists on paying the bills. Frankly, I don't think very damned much of men of that caliber, but then I'm a chauvinist."

"Of which you're exceedingly proud," she said sarcastically.

He laughed, conveying some cynicism. "Maybe so. Since no one's ever called me that before, I've had no reason to wonder about it." After a moment he asked, "Lola, is there anything besides sex that you like about me? Anything at all?"

Her entire body went rigid. "That's an insulting question."

"It's an honest question. Can you give me an honest answer?" What felt like an eternity passed with no answer from her at all. He drew in a long breath. "Guess you can't." Turning to the steering wheel, he put the shifting lever in Drive and got the car moving.

Her heart was pounding so fiercely, she marveled that he didn't hear it. There was a long list of things she liked about him. He was handsome, financially stable, intelligent—if with some pretty weird ideas about what he wanted in a wife—articulate, a respected citizen and sexy as sin.

But then he knew she thought he was sexy. It was the other things on her list he didn't know about. All she had to do was open her mouth and recite them, a simple enough feat. Why didn't she do it?

"People don't change, you know," she said instead.

"Pardon?"

"I said that people don't change. I'm talking about personalities and . . . and basic viewpoints. Even if both of us promised that we'd change after we were married, we really wouldn't."

Duke's badly deflated spirit began reviving. Maybe all was not lost.

"I'm sure you're right," he said cautiously. "But what if we changed *before* we got married?"

She cast a suspicious eye on him. "I'm not going to sell the store, Duke. And you don't want a working wife. What kind of changes are you talking about?"

"Damned if I know," he muttered. Again he wheeled to the side of the road. Only now they were in town. He parked under a huge old tree that was just sprouting leaves. Without preamble he slid across the seat and tipped her chin to look into her eyes. "I love you, I want you. If you feel the same about me, we'll find a way to work out our differences. What do you think?"

"I . . . I think marriage should be a partnership, not a dictatorship."

He strove for patience. "Okay, fine. But what do you think about us working through our differences?"

To her humiliation she began to cry. "I . . . don't . . . know," she wailed.

"Aw, hell," he mumbled, bringing her head to his chest. But then he thought he understood. "Honey, you've been through so much in the past week that your emotions are bound to be screwed up." He kissed the top of her head. "I don't know what else to say," he said, more to himself than to her.

Once again he slid back behind the wheel. In minutes he was pulling into her driveway.

From her purse she pulled out a tissue and blew her nose. "I don't know what to say, either," she told him, as though no time had elapsed since he'd said the same to her. "Except maybe we're not right for each other."

That was all he could take. His eyes hardened. "Do you want me to prove here and now just how really right we are for each other?"

"You're talking about sex."

"Damned right I'm talking about sex," he growled. "And don't sound so scornful. Sex is as important to you as it is to me, and, baby, we've got the real thing. Admit it, Lola. Face it."

Haughtily she lifted her chin. "The only thing I'll admit is that however important sex is, it's not a strong enough reason to get married. Good night."

He shook his head in dismay as she climbed out, slammed the door and all but ran to the back of the house.

He drove away thinking, *now what?*

Lola reopened the store and a week passed without a word from Duke. She was miserable, and what made it worse was knowing that all she had to do was pick up the phone and dial Duke's ranch to talk to him.

But how dare he make plans to sell her store without first talking to her about it? He'd made that announcement as though she should jump for joy to hear it.

She would never call him, she vowed. Never!

Duke was so grouchy, June told him off one day. And if ever there was a sweet-tempered woman, it was June Hansen. Afterward she apologized, he apologized and everything was okay between them, but Duke knew he couldn't go on like this. He was just barely sleeping and eating. His nerves were constantly on edge and he wondered if he wasn't getting an ulcer.

In desperation one afternoon, he called Charlie. "Could I impose on your good nature and ask you to meet me someplace? I really need some advice, Charlie."

"About Lola?"

"Yes. Would you help me out?"

"Glad to, Duke. The way she's been moping around, I'm willing to try anything to snap her out of it."

They met at a small diner on the edge of town. Seated in a booth, they ordered coffee.

Duke sipped from his cup. "You said Lola's been moping around?"

"Yes, but if you ever tell her I said it, I'll call you a liar. You know how I feel about that girl, and if it ever comes to taking sides, I'll be on hers."

"I understand." Duke set down his cup. "Charlie, I'm at my wit's end. She's all I think about, day and night. I asked her to marry me and she said no, even though she told me right out that she's in love with me. What in hell am I gonna do?"

"Told you she loves you, huh? Then said no to your marriage proposal? Doesn't add up, Duke." Charlie tasted his coffee and made a face. "Sure doesn't compare with the coffee I serve in my place."

Duke had to smile, but it didn't last long. "Charlie, why is Lola so determined to run that store?"

Charlie's eyes narrowed. "You didn't suggest she get rid of it, did you?"

"After we're married, yes. Charlie, I'm not in the Rockefeller class, but I'm far from being a poor man. I don't want my wife working."

Charlie shook his head. "You just answered your own question, Duke. The one about why she said no? If you want Lola, my friend, you'll have to take her just as she is."

Duke sat back. "In other words, I'd have to watch her drive off to work every day and wait for her to come home at night."

"Yep." Charlie cocked his head. "What's so terrible about that? I'm not being a smart-ass, Duke, I'm really interested in your answer."

Frowning, Duke pulled at his bottom lip with his thumb and forefinger. He finally lowered his hand. "I guess it's not terrible. It's just not how I visualized our marriage." He leaned forward. "Charlie, we could have such a great life. We could take trips and spend time together. *Do* things together. How can we do much of anything together with her gone six days a week?"

Charlie fell silent, obviously mulling it over. "I see where you're coming from, Duke. Listen, Lola's a very smart woman. I'm betting right here and now that it would take only a few weeks of living like that—if she really loves you— to change her mind about keeping the store."

"The last time we were together she said that people don't change," Duke said gloomily.

"Ah, but they do. They change a lot, believe me. I could tell you a story... But this is about you and Lola. You know what this whole thing depends on, Duke? On how willing you are to take a risk."

"What kind of risk?"

Charlie lowered his voice conspiratorially. "You tell her that you changed your mind about the store, and that she can keep it forever as far as you're concerned. She'll say yes and you'll get married. Then it happens. She has to leave you at the ranch very early every morning, and she doesn't get home until seven or eight every night. I'm betting she won't like it for long, Duke."

Duke mulled it over, then cleared his throat. "Wouldn't that be deceitful? I mean, deliberately lying to her about my feelings for the store?"

"Sure would," Charlie said cheerfully. He shrugged. "It's your life, my friend. How badly do you want Lola in it?"

"Lola? This is Duke."

She sank into her desk chair. Just hearing his voice was a thrill beyond measure.

"Hello, Duke. How are you?" she said calmly.

"Not very damned good without you, sweetheart. Will you see me tonight?"

It didn't take long for her to say "Yes."

"Seven okay?"

"I'll be ready."

After hanging up, she jumped up and let out a whoop, then peeked around the door of her office to see if anyone had heard her. No one was paying the slightest attention, thank goodness.

Hugging her arms around herself, she sat down again, put her head back, closed her eyes and fantasized about the night ahead.

Duke was prompt, and a few minutes after seven they were driving away from the house.

"Where are we going?" Lola asked.

"To the ranch."

"Oh."

He sent her a smile. "It's better than talking on the side of the road, sweetheart."

"Yes, of course." Her pulse was erratic. The ranch was also a better place to make love, and both of them knew that if he touched her even once they'd end up in bed. It was probably his ultimate goal, she thought without censure. After all, hadn't she been yearning for his kisses and caresses all week? Nixing marriage for the two of them didn't mean they couldn't see each other.

But there was a touch of sadness in her soul that their relationship had come to this. She herself had thought an affair with Duke was her best course, long before he had brought up the subject of marriage. He had probably come to the same conclusion.

Duke turned on the radio, and they listened to it with very little conversation during the drive. Duke did mention the great weather they were having, to which she could only agree, and that was about it. If there happened to be any topics on his agenda for the evening, he was saving them for when they were at the ranch, Lola decided. And the only things she could think of to talk about would cause dissension—the store, for instance.

Sighing quietly, she watched the road and listened to the music.

Finally parked near the ranch house, Duke took her hand and urged her to slide across the seat to get out on his side of the car. Then he surprised her with a kiss that went on and on. Breathless when it was over, she looked up at him.

"Damn, I missed you," he said raggedly.

"I missed you, too."

He cupped her face with his hands. "Did you?"

"Yes," she whispered. "I did."

He smiled. "That makes me very happy. Come on, let's go in." He took her hand for the walk into the house and to the living room. "Okay, what'll it be? Coffee, a soft drink? Some wine?" he said then.

"Hmm, nothing really. Thanks, anyway."

"I'm going to have some wine. Please join me."

"Well . . . all right." Lola perched on the edge of a sofa cushion, waiting for him to come back. He could have immediately led her to his bedroom and she would not have objected. He had to know that. So why, if making love was uppermost in his mind, had he brought her to the living room?

She eyed the fireplace, remembering their passion on the rug in front of the fire that one time. He could be thinking of something like that, she thought, even though tonight there was no fire on the grate. She added up the times they had made love, and the places, and her heart sank a little; they'd been involved in an affair almost from the first.

Duke returned with two glasses of wine, one of which he handed to her. He lifted his. "Cheers."

"Cheers," she echoed.

"Okay," he said after a healthy swallow of wine. "Now I'm ready for my little speech."

"Your speech?" she repeated with a startled expression.

"Will you listen to it?"

"Umm, yes, but..."

"Save the buts for later, okay?"

Perplexed, she hesitated, then nodded.

He cleared his throat and began walking back and forth in front of her. "It's like this, Lola. I love you and you love me. We should be together. We should be married. When I proposed, our hurdles to marriage were this. You wanted to keep your store and I wanted you to sell it. Well, I've done a lot of thinking this week and finally came to this conclusion. You were right and I was wrong. You're an independent woman and you're entitled to do whatever makes you happy. The store is no longer a problem for me, so I'm proposing again. Will you marry me?"

She was staring at him as though he had lost his mind. He grinned. "I've surprised you." He brought his glass to his lips and tossed back the rest of the wine in it.

Her own wine was barely touched. She was sitting board-stiff, trying to digest his "little speech."

Setting his glass down on a table, he seated himself next to her on the sofa. "So, what do you say? The hurdles are gone. Will you marry me now?"

"Duke..." Her voice was low and laden with tension. "Are you sure? I mean, are you really sure the store wouldn't be a problem? We discussed the difficulty of change, if you recall, and . . ."

"And I believe people *can* change. I've just proved it, in fact. You can keep your store until we're both old and gray. It simply doesn't matter anymore." All during his speech he'd been lying about that, so it was an enormous shock to his system to suddenly realize that he was no longer lying. So what if she worked? So what if she loved her store? She loved him more, he'd bet, and they would be together the way they were meant to be. They'd have every night, and every Sunday, and she would probably take a few weeks off once a year.

No, her store didn't mean a damned thing. What did was her and how much he loved her.

He took the glass from her trembling hand and set it aside, then turned her to face him. "I love you more than life itself," he said with great emotion. "Will you be my wife?"

Tears were spilling from her eyes. "Oh, Duke, I love you so much. Yes, I would be proud to be your wife. But how did this happen? What made you change your mind about the store?"

He grinned. "A little elf?"

She smiled through her tears. "Now you're being silly."

He put his arms around her and pulled her close. "I can't help being silly. Right now I feel like I could walk on air."

She snuggled closer to the heat of his body, recalling Serena's remarks about loving Edward so much she felt as though she were walking on air.

"I feel the same way, my love," she whispered. "Exactly the same."

Epilogue

They had a beautiful wedding in Charlie's church. Serena and Candace were Lola's attendants, and two friends of Duke's did the honors for him. After the ceremony, everyone—hordes of people—attended the reception held in Charlie's backyard. There were tables of food and drinks, and a live band. Charlie had constructed a small dance floor on the lawn, so there could be dancing.

Lola was radiant in a gorgeous ivory-colored gown, and Duke was resplendent in a formal, pale gray suit. It was the perfect wedding, and the bride and groom couldn't take their eyes off each other.

Charlie was in the middle of everything, but he took a moment to step back to observe and admire the happy couple. His little Lola was married. He had to blow his nose, the same as he'd had to do at Ron and Candace's wedding.

Losing his son was a blow he would never get over, but his grandson, Ronnie, was bringing him a great deal of happiness. "Thank you, God," he whispered. "Thank you for Ronnie."

He looked at Serena, his beautiful daughter, and at Candace, whom he'd come to love as his own. He was a lucky man.

Then his gaze drifted over the crowd of laughing, chattering friends. Yes, indeed, he was a very lucky man.

Everything was as close to perfect as life allowed.

A young woman wearing dark glasses, a lovely teal dress and matching accessories hovered on the edge of the crowd. She was becoming bolder; being here was evidence of her developing confidence.

The day was coming when she would be ready for what she'd come to Rocky Ford to do. Only she would know when the time was right.

She sipped from her glass of wine and studied Charlie through the dark lenses concealing her eyes.

Yes, she would know when the time was right.

It wasn't today. Setting her glass on a nearby table, she quietly slipped away.

* * * * *

Serena finds love—and the mystery woman makes
a move—in Book Two of Made in Montana,
Montana Passion. Coming next month in
Silhouette Special Edition.

The first book in the exciting new
Fortune's Children series is
HIRED HUSBAND
by *New York Times* bestselling writer
Rebecca Brandewyne

Beginning in July 1996
Only from Silhouette Books

Here's an exciting sneak preview....

Minneapolis, Minnesota

As Caroline Fortune wheeled her dark blue Volvo into the underground parking lot of the towering, glass-and-steel structure that housed the global headquarters of Fortune Cosmetics, she glanced anxiously at her gold Piaget wristwatch. An accident on the snowy freeway had caused rush-hour traffic to be a nightmare this morning. As a result, she was running late for her 9:00 a.m. meeting—and if there was one thing her grandmother, Kate Winfield Fortune, simply couldn't abide, it was slack, unprofessional behavior on the job. And lateness was the sign of a sloppy, disorganized schedule.

Involuntarily, Caroline shuddered at the thought of her grandmother's infamous wrath being unleashed upon her. The stern rebuke would be precise, apropos, scathing and delivered with coolly raised, condemnatory eyebrows and in icy tones of haughty grandeur that had in the past reduced many an executive—even the male ones—at Fortune Cosmetics not only to obsequious apologies, but even to tears. Caroline had seen it happen on more than one occasion, although, much to her gratitude and relief, she herself was seldom a target of her grandmother's anger. And she wouldn't be this morning, either, not if she could help it. That would be a disastrous way to start out the new year.

Grabbing her Louis Vuitton totebag and her black leather portfolio from the front passenger seat, Caroline stepped gracefully from the Volvo and slammed the door. The heels of her Maud Frizon pumps clicked briskly on the concrete floor as she hurried toward the bank of elevators that would take her up into the skyscraper owned by her family. As the elevator doors slid open, she rushed down the long, plushly carpeted corridors of one of the hushed upper floors toward the conference room.

By now Caroline had her portfolio open and was leafing through it as she hastened along, reviewing her notes she had prepared for her presentation. So she didn't see Dr. Nicolai Valkov until she literally ran right into him. Like her, he had his head bent over his own portfolio, not watching where he was going. As the two of them collided, both their portfolios and the papers inside went flying. At the unexpected impact, Caroline lost her balance, stumbled, and would have fallen had not Nick's strong, sure hands abruptly shot out, grabbing hold of her and pulling her to him to steady her. She gasped, startled and stricken, as she came up hard against his broad chest, lean hips and corded thighs, her face just inches from his own—as though they were lovers about to kiss.

Caroline had never been so close to Nick Valkov before, and, in that instant, she was acutely aware of him—not just as a fellow employee of Fortune Cosmetics but also as a man. Of how tall and ruggedly handsome he was, dressed in an elegant, pin-striped black suit cut in the European fashion, a crisp white shirt, a foulard tie and a pair of Cole Haan loafers. Of how dark his thick, glossy hair and his deep-set eyes framed by raven-wing brows were—so dark that they were almost black, despite the bright, fluorescent lights that blazed overhead. Of the whiteness of his straight teeth against his bronzed skin as a brazen, mocking grin slowly curved his wide, sensual mouth.

"Actually, I *was* hoping for a sweet roll this morning—but I daresay you would prove even tastier, Ms. Fortune," Nick drawled impertinently, his low, silky voice tinged with a faint accent born of the fact that Russian, not English, was his native language.

At his words, Caroline flushed painfully, embarrassed and annoyed. If there was one person she always attempted to avoid at Fortune Cosmetics, it was Nick Valkov. Following the breakup of the Soviet Union, he had emigrated to the United States, where her grandmother had hired him to direct the company's research and development department. Since that time, Nick had constantly demonstrated marked, traditional, Old World tendencies that had led Caroline to believe he not only had no use for equal rights but also would actually have been more than happy to turn back the clock several centuries where females were concerned. She thought his remark was typical of his attitude toward women: insolent, arrogant and domineering. Really, the man was simply insufferable!

Caroline couldn't imagine what had ever prompted her grandmother to hire him—and at a highly generous salary, too—except that Nick Valkov was considered one of the foremost chemists anywhere on the planet. Deep down inside Caroline knew that no matter how he behaved, Fortune Cosmetics was extremely lucky to have him. Still, that didn't give him the right to manhandle and insult her!

"I assure you that you would find me more bitter than a cup of the strongest black coffee, Dr. Valkov," she insisted, attempting without success to free her trembling body from his steely grip, while he continued to hold her so near that she could feel his heart beating steadily in his chest—and knew he must be equally able to feel the erratic hammering of her own.

"Oh, I'm willing to wager there's more sugar and cream to you than you let on, Ms. Fortune." To her utter mortification and outrage, she felt one of Nick's hands slide insidiously up her back and nape to her luxuriant mass of sable hair, done up in a stylish French twist.

"You know so much about fashion," he murmured, eyeing her assessingly, pointedly ignoring her indignation and efforts to escape from him. "So why do you always wear your hair like this... so tightly wrapped and severe? I've never seen it down. Still, that's the way it needs to be worn, you know... soft, loose, tangled about your face. As it is, your hair fairly cries out for a man to take the pins from it, so he can see how long it is. Does it fall past your shoulders?'' He quirked one eyebrow inquisitively, a mocking half smile still twisting his lips, letting her know he was enjoying her obvious discomfiture. ''You aren't going to tell me, are you? What a pity. Because my guess is that it does— and I'd like to know if I'm right. And these glasses.'' He indicated the large, square, tortoiseshell frames perched on her slender, classic nose. ''I think you use them to hide behind more than you do to see. I'll bet you don't actually even need them at all.''

Caroline felt the blush that had yet to leave her cheeks deepen, its heat seeming to spread throughout her entire quivering body. Damn the man! Why must he be so infuriatingly perceptive?

Because everything that Nick suspected was true.

* * * * *

To read more, don't miss
HIRED HUSBAND
by Rebecca Brandewyne,
Book One in the new
FORTUNE'S CHILDREN *series,*
beginning this month and available only from
Silhouette Books!

MILLION DOLLAR SWEEPSTAKES

A Funny Thing Happened on the Way to the Baby Shower...

When four college friends reunite to celebrate the arrival of one bouncing baby, they find four would-be grooms on the way!

Don't miss a single, sexy tale in

RAYE MORGAN'S

Only in

BABY DREAMS
in May '96 (SD #997)

A GIFT FOR BABY
in July '96 (SD #1010)

BABIES BY THE BUSLOAD
in September '96 (SD #1022)

And look for

INSTANT DAD, WILL TRAIN
in November '96

Only from

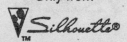

RMBS

Silhouette's recipe for a sizzling summer:

* Take the best-looking cowboy in South Dakota
* Mix in a brilliant bachelor
* Add a sexy, mysterious sheikh
* Combine their stories into one collection and you've got one sensational super-hot read!

Three short stories by these favorite authors:

Kathleen Eagle
Joan Hohl
Barbara Faith

Available this July wherever
Silhouette books are sold.

New York Times Bestselling Author
REBECCA BRANDEWYNE

Launches a new twelve-book series—FORTUNE'S CHILDREN
beginning in July 1996 with Book One

Hired Husband

Caroline Fortune knew her marriage to Nick Valkov was in
name only. She would help save the family business, Nick
would get a green card, and a paper marriage would suit both
of them. Until Caroline could no longer deny the feelings Nick
stirred in her and the practical union turned passionate.

MEET THE FORTUNES—a family whose legacy is greater than
riches. Because where there's a will...there's a wedding!

Look for Book Two, *The Millionaire and the Cowgirl*,
by Lisa Jackson. Available in August 1996 wherever Silhouette
books are sold.

This exciting new cross-line continuity series unites five of your favorite authors as they weave five connected novels about love, marriage—and Daddy's unexpected need for a baby carriage!

Get ready for

THE BABY NOTION by Dixie Browning (SD#1011, 7/96)
Single gal Priscilla Barrington would do anything for a baby—even visit the local sperm bank. Until cowboy Jake Spencer set out to convince her to have a family the natural—and much more exciting—way!

And the romance in New Hope, Texas, continues with:

BABY IN A BASKET
by Helen R. Myers (SR#1169, 8/96)

MARRIED...WITH TWINS!
by Jennifer Mikels (SSE#1054, 9/96)

HOW TO HOOK A HUSBAND (AND A BABY)
by Carolyn Zane (YT#29, 10/96)

DISCOVERED: DADDY
by Marilyn Pappano (IM#746, 11/96)

DADDY KNOWS LAST arrives in July...only from

DKL-D

You're About to Become a

Privileged Woman

Reap the rewards of fabulous free gifts and benefits with proofs-of-purchase from Silhouette and Harlequin books

Pages & Privileges™

It's our way of thanking you for buying our books at your favorite retail stores.

PROOF OF PURCHASE

SD-PP156

Offer expires October 31, 1996

Pages & Privileges ™

**Harlequin and Silhouette—
the most privileged readers in the world!**

For more information about Harlequin and Silhouette's PAGES & PRIVILEGES program call the Pages & Privileges Benefits Desk: 1-503-794-2499

Silhouette®

SD-PP156